L'ASSOMMOIR

A stage version of the novel

by
ÉMILE ZOLA

Adapted by
STEPHEN WYATT

With
JANE GIBSON and
SUE LEFTON

With lyrics by
ANTHONY INGLE and
STEPHEN WYATT

And music by

ANTHONY INGLE

This version of L'Assommoir was premiered as A
Working Woman at the West Yorkshire Playhouse in
Leeds in November 1992.

Characters:

In the Leeds production, the play was performed by a cast of eleven - six women and five men - plus a musician. The parts were divided in this way:

- GERVAISE
- NANA / CLEMENCE / GRAND LADY AT THE LOUVRE / WASHERWOMAN / CHORUS
- VIRGINIE / LEONIE / ÉTIENNE / GRAND LADY AT THE LOUVRE / PROSTITUTE / CHORUS
- MME GOUJET / MME LERAT / MME PUTOIS / OLD WOMAN / WASHERWOMAN / CHORUS
- MME LORILLEUX / ADELE / CLOTHILDE / AUGUSTINE / WASHERWOMAN / CHORUS
- MME BOCHE / MA COUPEAU / LAUNDRESS AT MME FAUCONNIER'S / CHORUS

- COUPEAU / CHORUS
- LANTIER / MADINIER / FOUNDRY WORKER / MAN IN STREET / CHORUS
- GOUJET / MES BOTTES / KEEPER / WASHERWOMAN / CHORUS
- BEC SALÉ / LORILLEUX / DOCTOR / MAN IN STREET / WASHERWOMAN / CHORUS
- BAZOUGE / POISSON / BIBI LA GRILLADE / FOUNDRY WORKER / PRIEST / ATTENDANT AT THE LOUVRE / CHARLES (WASHHOUSE) / NANA'S ADMIRER / MAN IN STREET / CHORUS

Alternative ways of dividing the parts are, of course, possible.

<u>Setting</u>:

PARIS - between 1850 and 1869

ACT ONE

*
—

AN EMPTY CAFÉ-CONCERT.
THE MUSICIAN BEGINS TO PLAY.
THE ACTORS ENTER CASUALLY
AND TAKE UP POSITIONS.
THEN THEY COME INTO THE MAIN
SPACE.
THEY DANCE A WILD, FRENETIC
CAN-CAN.
GERVAISE APPEARS, A FIGURE
APART, RAISED UP, WAITING,
MOVING WITH A PRONOUNCED
LIMP.
THE OTHERS START TO LEAVE -
APART FROM LANTIER AND
ADELE WHO DANCE ON.
THEN THEY TOO LEAVE.
GERVAISE WATCHES ADELE AND
LANTIER AS THEY GO.
THEN ALL THAT REMAINS IS
GERVAISE WAITING.
ETIENNE IS ASLEEP NEARBY.

MORNING LIGHT. GERVAISE STILL
WAITS.
COUPEAU LOOKS IN ON GERVAISE.

COUPEAU:	Old man not home then, Madame Lantier?
GERVAISE:	No, he isn't, Monsieur Coupeau.

GERVAISE TRIES TO RETURN
COUPEAU'S SMILE.

COUPEAU:	The door was open and I thought I'd just pop my head round. I'm working over at

5

the hospital now, you know. Lovely morning to be tiling a roof, isn't it?

HE LINGERS - TAKING IN THE SLEEPING CHILD, THE UNSLEPT IN BED, GERVAISE'S TEAR-STAINED FACE.

COUPEAU: Well, well, the old man's not been behaving himself then? It's the politics, isn't it? I expect he's been out all night putting the world to rights with his mates - complaining about that bastard Napoleon.

GERVAISE: I know where he is, Monsieur Coupeau.

COUPEAU: Look, if you don't want to go out, I could get your milk for you.

GERVAISE: (SHAKING HER HEAD) No, no, please don't bother. Claude's gone for it.

COUPEAU: It's no bother - not for you. (A SLIGHTLY AWKWARD PAUSE) Anyway, you know you can always count on me if you need anything.

HE FINALLY LEAVES.
THEN MADAME BOCHE APPEARS AND CALLS UP.

MME B: Here, Madame Lantier, you're up early.

GERVAISE: (LOOKING DOWN) Oh, Madame Boche - I've got a lot to do today.

MME B: Your lord and master up yet, is he?

GERVAISE: No, no, he's still asleep.

MME B: Lucky for some! I'll save you a place at the washhouse. We can have a proper chat then.

GERVAISE NODS FAINTLY.

MME B:	(MORE KINDLY) You'd better get back inside, dear, you look terrible.
	MADAME BOCHE GOES. GERVAISE SITS. SHE FINALLY BEGINS TO DOZE OFF. THEN LANTIER WALKS IN. SHE OPENS HER EYES AND SEES HIM THERE.
GERVAISE:	(RISING) It's you, it's you!
LANTIER:	Yes, it's me. What about it? Don't start all that.
GERVAISE:	Where have you been?
LANTIER:	Out with my mate - the one's who's starting up his own hat factory. Alright?
GERVAISE:	(TRYING TO EMBRACE HIM) Auguste, where have you been? Please, please tell me where you've been. Where did you spend the night?
LANTIER:	I don't have to answer to you. Just get off me, get off me, woman. I don't have to fucking well answer to you.
	THE QUARREL HAS AWOKEN ETIENNE. HE STARTS TO CRY. GERVAISE GOES TO COMFORT HIM.
LANTIER:	Oh, God, here comes the music! Now look what you've done. I can't stand this. I'm off.
GERVAISE:	(RUNNING TO HIM AGAIN) No, no -
LANTIER:	Jesus, what a dump! (LOOKING AT HER) And I suppose you've given up washing your face?
GERVAISE:	I'd like to see you do better. You try bringing up two kids in this place with

7

	nowhere to boil the water. You should have found us somewhere decent to live when we came to Paris instead of wasting all our money on nothing.
LANTIER:	I didn't notice you were averse to helping me spend it.
GERVAISE:	Look, we got ourselves into this mess and we can get ourselves out of it. I can start work with Madame Fauconnier at the laundry on Monday. If you could start with your mate at his hat factory, we could make it, I know we could.
LANTIER:	(TURNING AWAY, BORED) Give me strength.
GERVAISE:	(ANGERED) You don't want to work but you want the money so you can dance about with tarts in silk skirts. I know where you were last night and I know who you were with - that stuck-up bitch Adele. Yeah, she can afford to look nice. She's slept with the whole street. (LANTIER TURNS ANGRILY) Oh yes, the whole street.

HE GRABS HER AND STARTS TO SHAKE HER. ETIENNE STARTS TO CRY AGAIN.

LANTIER:	You've done it, Gervaise, you've really done it now.

GERVAISE COMFORTS HER SON, STROKING HIS HEAD.
LANTIER SITS WAITING.
GERVAISE FINALLY RISES AND GATHERS UP THE WASHING.

LANTIER:	What are you up to? (NO ANSWER. FIERCER) Going out?

GERVAISE:	All this needs washing. The kids can't live in filth like this.
LANTIER:	Got any money?
GERVAISE:	Why?
LANTIER:	I thought I told you to hock some stuff yesterday, didn't I?
GERVAISE:	I could hock the kids for all you care.
LANTIER:	For Christ's sake, how much did you get?
GERVAISE:	(AFTER A PAUSE) Five sous. That's every spare scrap of clothing I had. Now there's nothing left to hock. And we owe the dairy a week.

HE SILENTLY HOLDS OUT HIS HAND.
SHE HANDS THE MONEY OVER.

GERVAISE:	While I'm away, will you get us some bread?
LANTIER:	Yes.

SHE OPENS A TRUNK AND STARTS TO TAKE OUT SHIRTS.

LANTIER:	Leave my things alone.
GERVAISE:	You want your shirts washing, don't you?
LANTIER:	Leave them alone.
GERVAISE:	You can't put those filthy things on again.
LANTIER:	Christ Almighty, do what I say just this once.
GERVAISE:	(SHE STARES AT HIM) You're not going away, are you?
LANTIER:	(MOCK PATIENT) Look, I just don't want you going about telling everybody you keep me by taking in washing and mending. Alright? I'll do my own stuff.
GERVAISE:	Please -

GERVAISE HESITATES THEN REPLACES THE SHIRTS.

LANTIER: Look, I'm tired, just stop nagging and let me sleep.

GERVAISE: (TURNING TO HER SON) Etienne, daddy wants to sleep. When Claude comes back, you boys play quietly.

ETIENNE: Yes.

GERVAISE TURNS BACK TO LANTIER BUT HIS EYES ARE CLOSED.
SHE LEAVES. LANTIER RISES AND EYES THE TRUNK.
HE SITS ON IT THOUGHTFULLY.
AS HE DOES SO, MADAME BOCHE AND THE WASHERWOMEN START TO APPEAR WITH THEIR WASHING.
LANTIER PICKS UP THE TRUNK AND LEAVES.

**

THE WASH HOUSE. AS THE WOMEN SETTLE TO THEIR WORK, THEY GREET EACH OTHER AND PEOPLE IN THE AUDIENCE:

Morning, Madame Boche, how are you?
Can't complain, and yourself?
You're looking better than when I last saw you.
Haven't seen you for a few weeks. You alright?
Oh, didn't spot you over there. Bit early for you, isn't it?

10

Better get on, can't stand here talking all day.

WHEN THEY'RE FINALLY SETTLED INTO THE RHYTHM OF THEIR WASHING, THE WOMEN START TO GOSSIP.

The fourth floor couple were at it again.
At what?
Fighting, of course. What did you think?
Every day it's the same. He beats her. She kicks him.
He's the pisshead?
Out of his skull every night. Mind you, I blame her too.
Why's that?
She's got the filthiest tongue. It's fucking this and fucking that all fucking night. At the top of her fucking voice. Drives you round the fucking bend.
Give me a break. Do me a favour.

That tart's got her marching orders.
The one upstairs?
That's the one. And not for what you'd think. Landlord doesn't give a fuck who does what.
So long as he gets his money.
That's right. She could have the whole fucking army in there for all he cares.
So long as she pays the rent.
That's right.
So what happened?
She can't pay the fucking rent. That's what's happened. Mind you, she's thirty five if she's a day. And ugly as sin.
Do me a favour. Give me a break.

11

IN THE MIDDLE OF THIS DIN,
GERVAISE ARRIVES.
CHARLES, THE MALE ATTENDANT,
SPOTS HER.

CHARLES: Number fifty-three.

SHE LOOKS AROUND FOR
MADAME BOCHE. SHE SPOTS HER
AND GOES OVER.
MADAME BOCHE KEEPS ON
RUBBING A SOCK AS SHE TALKS.

MME B: Stick yourself there. I've kept you a
place. I won't be long. Boche hardly
dirties a thing.

GERVAISE OPENS HER BUNDLE OF
WASHING.

MME B: Well, that won't take long either, will it?
Here you need a pail of soda for the boys'
shirts.
GERVAISE: No, hot water'll do.
MME B: I forget. I'm talking to the professional.
(SHE WATCHES GERVAISE
WASHING) God, you've got strong
arms.
GERVAISE: I've been doing this since I was ten. Back
home we used to take it to the river.
Smelt better than it does here.
MME B: I bet it did.
GERVAISE: It was a lovely spot. Under the trees.
With clear, running water. In Plassans.
Near Marseille. (PAUSE) Then Lantier
decided it was time for a move.

12

SHE WORKS ON. THE OTHER WOMEN CONTINUE TO TALK AS THEY WASH:

WOMEN: Look at the stains on that -
God knows how he does it -
And he wants his collars clean -
Or there'll be trouble.
Get a load of the smell of this -
Christ, it's fucking evil -
Pissed again last night -
And it's all down the front.
How can you love a man
Once you've scrubbed his shitty clothes?
Just once I'd like to fuck a gent
Whose knickers wouldn't smell of shit.
My kid's not well, look at this -
You don't think it's blood
I've lost three already
And I don't want to lose him -
Look at the stains
Smell the stench
Scrub off the filth
And wash away the shit.

GERVAISE AND MADAME BOCHE START TO TALK AGAIN AS GERVAISE TAKES HER BEATER TO THE CLOTHES.

MME B: (EVER CURIOUS) How is Lantier?
GERVAISE: (BEATING CLOTHES FIERCELY AS SHE TALKS :) He's impossible since we came to Paris. He's spent all the money his mother left him. I can't bring the children up on nothing, I just can't. He was going to set me up in a laundry and he was going to get work and we were going to be happy. (PAUSE) I'd be better

13

off back home being beaten black and blue by my father.

THE MALE ATTENDANT COMES FORWARD.

CHARLES: There's a boy here asking for his mum.

ETIENNE COMES FORWARD SHYLY, AWARE OF ALL THE WOMEN STARING. GERVAISE DROPS HER WASHING AS SHE SEES HIM.

GERVAISE: Etienne - (HE RUNS OVER) Has Dad sent you?
ETIENNE: Dad's gone.
GERVAISE: Yes, he's gone out to buy bread, I know.
ETIENNE: No, he's gone. He jumped off the bed, he took the trunk and he's gone in a cab...

HE HOLDS UP A KEY. GERVAISE STARES AT IT.

GERVAISE: Oh god, oh god, oh god ...
MME B: (BUTTING IN) So Daddy told you to shut the door and you and your brother came here with the key. Is that right?
ETIENNE: He took the trunk and he's gone in a cab.
MME B: And was there a lady in the cab?

ETIENNE DOESN'T ANSWER.

GERVAISE: Go home now. I'll be back soon.

ETIENNE RUNS OFF.
MME BOCHE WANTS TO ASK MORE BUT A LOOK AT GERVAISE'S FACE STOPS HER.

14

GERVAISE IS GASPING FOR
BREATH.

GERVAISE: You don't know the half of it... He took
my last five sous... I paid for that cab....
My clothes paid for that cab...
MME B: He's not worth it, love. They're all the
same. Why us women ever get married, I
don't know -
GERVAISE: (CUTTING IN) We're not married.
MME B: Married or not, you're still better off
without him.

GERVAISE STANDS STUNNED.
VIRGINIE ENTERS WITH A TOKEN
QUANTITY OF WASHING. SHE
WALKS SLOWLY DOWN PAST
GERVAISE, SMILING, AND THEN
BACK UP TO A PLACE WITH THE
OTHER WASHERWOMEN.

CHARLES: Number fifty-four.
MME B: Don't look now but Virginie's here.
Adele's sister.
WASHERWOMAN: Hey, Virginie, what are you doing
here?

VIRGINIE PULLS A COUPLE OF
OTHER WOMEN INTO A HUDDLE
FOR A WHISPER. HER FACE IS FULL
OF MALICIOUS AMUSEMENT.

MME B: (LOOKING AT HER) I reckon she's only
come here to gloat. She knows all about
it, you can bet your life. She's going to
run straight home and tell them how
you've taken it.

A BURST OF LAUGHTER FROM
VIRGINIE AND HER FRIENDS.
GERVAISE TURNS TO FACE
VIRGINIE. VIRGINIE IS AWARE OF
HER GAZE.

VIRGINIE: (TO HER FRIENDS) I think Lantier
              prefers his women with two legs.

              GERVAISE PICKS UP THE BUCKET
              AND THROWS THE WATER AT HER.

VIRGINIE: You bitch!

              THE WHOLE WASHHOUSE IS
              SILENT NOW. VIRGINIE TURNS
              ANGRILY.

VIRGINIE: So what made you do that then, you
              lopsided cow?
GERVAISE: (HOTLY) As if you didn't know.
VIRGINIE: It's not me that's taken your precious
              husband. Anyone here found Madame's
              husband? I'm sure she'll offer a reward.
GERVAISE: He's gone with your sister, you know
              bloody well.
VIRGINIE: And who can blame him?
GERVAISE: You cow, you bloody cow!

              SHE ATTACKS VIRGINIE. THE TWO
              WOMEN ROLL ACROSS THE FLOOR
              FIGHTING WHILE THE OTHER
              WOMEN ENCOURAGE THEM AND
              BEAT THEIR BUCKETS AND
              BOARDS EXCITEDLY.

MME B: (TO CHARLES) Someone ought to stop
              them.

CHARLES: (GRINNING) Not me, love. Best show I've seen in years.

GERVAISE GRABS VIRGINIE'S EAR AND PULLS HER EARRING OFF.
VIRGINIE SCREAMS AT THE PAIN THEN GRABS GERVAISE AND WRENCHES HER ARM SAVAGELY BEHIND HER BACK.
TRIUMPHANTLY SHE CLAIMS VICTORY.
BUT GERVAISE COMES UP BEHIND HER AND FORCES HER OVER ONE OF THE IRONING BOARDS.
SHE GRABS A WOODEN BEATER FROM ONE OF THE OTHER WOMEN, PULLS DOWN VIRGINIE'S DRAWERS AND STARTS TO BEAT HER.

GERVAISE: I'll tan your arse for you! You won't sit down for a week!

THE OTHER WOMEN ROAR APPROVAL AND DANCE MOCKINGLY ROUND THE BEATING TO CAN-CAN MUSIC.
FINALLY GERVAISE, EXHAUSTED AND SATISFIED, THROWS DOWN THE BEATER.
VIRGINIE CRAWLS AWAY, SOBBING WITH HUMILIATION.
THE OTHERS CONGRATULATE GERVAISE AND THEN START TO LEAVE.
GERVAISE STANDS THERE, THE EXCITEMENT OF HER MOMENT OF TRIUMPH SEEPING FROM HER.

SOMEONE HANDS HER HER BUNDLE OF WASHING.
GERVAISE IS ALONE WITH HER BUNDLE OF WASHING.

***

LIGHTS CHANGE. COUPEAU COMES IN. HE SMILES AS HE SEES HER.

COUPEAU: How's the laundry job?
GERVAISE: It's a job. It's put me back on my feet.
COUPEAU: Fancy a drink?
GERVAISE: Just a small one then. (PAUSE) But it's still no, Monsieur Coupeau.
COUPEAU: I haven't asked you again yet.
GERVAISE: Look, I'm a working woman with two kids to feed. I'm telling you I wouldn't make you happy.
COUPEAU: Oh, come over here and say that again.
GERVAISE: I don't know what you want a cripple for.
COUPEAU: Come on, let's have that drink.

HE LEADS HER TO A BAR TABLE. OTHER MEN LEAN AGAINST THE BAR SEAT DRINKING, THEIR BACKS TO THE AUDIENCE.

COUPEAU: Brandy plum?

HE PLACES THE DRINK IN FRONT OF HER AS THEY SIT.

COUPEAU: Anyway, you've seen the last of Lantier, I suppose?

18

GERVAISE: He's supposed to be living with that Adele at his mate's place. Not that I care. I'm better off on my own.

COUPEAU: Yeah, but there are some things you can't do better on your own, aren't there?

GERVAISE: You know your trouble, Coupeau? You've got sex on the brain.

COUPEAU: Funny place to have it.

BUT HIS SMILE FADES AND HE STARES LONGINGLY AT HER.

GERVAISE: Look, Monsieur Coupeau, I'm sorry. But I've got a home to run. I've got a job to do. I haven't got time for fun and games.

COUPEAU: (ADMIRINGLY) You're so brave, you're so strong.

GERVAISE: I'm not. Anyone can push me around. I hate upsetting people. But it's just not right.

SHE RISES TO LEAVE BUT HE STOPS HER.

COUPEAU: (TOUCHING HER) It feels alright to me. Come on, sit down. I'm not going to leap on you, you know. There's a table between us. I'd do myself an injury.

SHE SMILES AT THIS AND SITS AGAIN.
MES-BOTTES DETACHES HIMSELF FROM THE GROUP OF DRINKING MEN AND APPROACHES. HE'S CLEARLY FAIRLY DRUNK.

MES-BOTTES: Well, if it isn't old Coupeau - looking very smart.

COUPEAU: (EMBARRASSED) Mes-Bottes!

MES-B:	Trying to impress the little lady, are you? (TO GERVAISE) I'm one of his oldest friends though you wouldn't think it.
COUPEAU:	Leave me alone.
MES-B:	Who do you think you are? (MUTTERING AS HE TURNS AWAY) What a shit! Doesn't want to know me now.

PEEVED, MES-BOTTES REJOINS HIS MATES.

COUPEAU:	Sorry.
GERVAISE:	My mum used to drink - and I drank with her. I stopped the day I nearly died of it. I can't bear the stuff any more. (SHE HOLDS UP THE GLASS) Just the plum, you see. I don't touch the booze.
COUPEAU:	I'm the same. My mates give me stick for not joining in but it doesn't bother me. (MORE CONFIDENTIAL :) My dad was a tiler too, you see. Well, one day he went on the job really pissed. Fell through the roof and killed himself.
GERVAISE:	I'm sorry.
COUPEAU_	Don't be. It taught us all a lesson - and it didn't do the roof much good either. So just one plum brandy and that's it. You need steady legs in my job.
GERVAISE:	(NODDING) I must go.

AS SHE REACHES FOR HER WASHING, SHE STOPS AND RESTS IT IN HER LAP.

GERVAISE:	God knows I'm not ambitious. I don't ask for very much. My dream is to get on quietly with my work, always to have something to eat and a decent place to

20

	sleep. A bed, a table and a couple of chairs, that's all. I'd like to bring up my kids to be decent people. And, if I took up with somebody again, I wouldn't want to be beaten. I've had enough of that for one lifetime. (PAUSE) And, at the end, after working and slaving all my life, I'd like to die at home in my own bed.
COUPEAU:	Waste of a good bed if that's all you're going to do in it.
GERVAISE:	Now don't start that again.

AS THEY RISE, THE MEN AT THE BAR START TO SHOUT AT COLOMBE:

MEN:	- Come on, Colombe. shift your arse. - My tongue's hanging out. - When are we going to get some service? - Come on Colombe, we need a drink.

ON THE WAY OUT, COUPEAU TURNS TO GERVAISE, SUDDENLY SERIOUS.

COUPEAU:	I'll never drink, Gervaise, I'll never beat you. I love you too much.

AS THEY LEAVE, THE MEN IN THE BAR TURN AND SING:

Let's go to another bar, let's chuck this one in
Find somewhere they'll serve you, the same day you go in.
We're good honest workers, the salt of the earth
And a little relaxation is what we deserve.

THE MEN LEAVE THE BAR STILL
SINGING.
LIGHTS CHANGE. GERVAISE SITS
SEWING OVERALLS. KNOCK.
COUPEAU ENTERS.

COUPEAU: I've brought you your milk.
GERVAISE: Thanks.

HE PUTS IT DOWN AND PAUSES.

COUPEAU: Don't you ever stop working?
GERVAISE: I've got three mouths to feed.
COUPEAU: You need to rest sometimes.
GERVAISE: Look, my mum and dad boozed their
            lives away in front of my eyes.   And
            that's not happening to me.
COUPEAU: Come on, Gervaise, have a little lie down
            with me.

HE TRIES TO KISS HER. SHE PULLS
AWAY.
HE GRABS HER AND SHE REACTS
VIOLENTLY.

GERVAISE: Get off me.

SHE PUSHES HIM AND COUPEAU
FALLS.

COUPEAU: Ah, the power in those arms. I don't stand
            a chance, do I?

DESPITE HERSELF, SHE LAUGHS.

COUPEAU: It's no joke, you know.
GERVAISE: You'll get over it. (SHE HANDS HIM
            HIS OVERALLS) Sorry, I've the kids'
            supper to get.

HE STARTS TO MOVE AWAY.

COUPEAU: Thanks for the sewing.

AS HE LEAVES, THE MEN CROSS
THE STAGE AGAIN DRUNKENLY
SINGING: 'Let's go to another bar...'

LIGHTS. GERVAISE IS AGAIN IN
HER ROOM, WORKING. IT'S LATE.
SHE LOOKS UP. COUPEAU STANDS
THERE, SHAKING AND CRYING.

COUPEAU: Gervaise?
GERVAISE: Yes?
COUPEAU: Gervaise -
GERVAISE: Yes?
COUPEAU: This can't go on, can it? I haven't slept for three nights. (PAUSE) I've decided. We've got to get married.
GERVAISE: Monsieur Coupeau, you don't know what you're saying. Maybe if you didn't see so much of me you'd get over it. Men often get married for just one thing. Then spend the rest of their lives regretting it. We're better off as we are.
COUPEAU: But I want you. Really want you. You're hurting me very much.
GERVAISE: What will people say? It's only two months since I was with Lantier - and we weren't even married. You don't want to have to bring up his kids.
COUPEAU: You're so brave, so kind. I'll never find another woman like you.

GERVAISE SHAKES HER HEAD. AN
ACCORDION STARTS TO PLAY.

23

COUPEAU: I want you.
GERVAISE: Oh, you are a nuisance.
COUPEAU: Say yes - please.
GERVAISE: (FINALLY) Oh, alright, then - yes.

AS COUPEAU GOES TO KISS AND
EMBRACE HER, DRUNKEN
SHOUTING IS HEARD IN THE
DARKNESS.

DRUNK: What the fuck's going on? Where the
                fuck am I?

****

LIGHTS CHANGE.
THE INHABITANTS OF THE
TENEMENT APPEAR - EACH WITH
THEIR OWN BALCONY RAILING.
THEY SHOUT TO EACH OTHER
AMIDST THE DIN.

DRUNK: (TO HIS WIFE) Don't you tell me what
                to do, you fucking cow.
WOMAN: (NURSING HER CRYING BABY)
                You've woke my baby up again.
PROSTITUTE: (CALLING DOWN) Come back, you
                cheating bastard, give me the rest of
                my money.
MADINIER: (CALLING UP TO HER) Shut up!
EVERYBODY ELSE: (CALLING DOWN TO HIM) Shut
                up yourself.

GERVAISE AND COUPEAU ENTER.
HE GESTURES FOR HER TO
FOLLOW. SHE HESITATES.

COUPEAU: Come on, Gervaise.

GERVAISE: I don't see why we have to.

COUPEAU: I've got to see my sister and her husband.

GERVAISE: Why?

COUPEAU: They'll be missing my money now I won't be eating with them any more. Not that they don't earn more than both of us put together. But, still, I'd like them to give us their blessing.

GERVAISE: Your ma has.

COUPEAU: That's different.

GERVAISE: Alright, if it's that important.

COUPEAU: (KISSING HER) Anyway, I bet you've never seen gold chain being made before.

GERVAISE: So they've really got gold there?

COUPEAU: On the walls, on the floor, all over the shop. Come on.

THEY REACH THE TENEMENT.
THEY LOOK UP. GERVAISE GASPS.

COUPEAU: Sixth floor. It's quite a hike.

GERVAISE: But it's huge.

SHE STARES UP AT THE TENEMENT BLOCK.
THE NOISE OF THE TENEMENT RETURNS.
MADINIER WHO'S AT THE FRONT TURNS AND SEES COUPEAU.

MADINIER: Morning, Coupeau.

GERVAISE AND COUPEAU START TO WALK UP THE BUILDING.
AS THEY GO UP, THE INHABITANTS OF THE TENEMENT LEAVE, SHOUTING OR COMPLAINING AS THEY GO.

25

PROSTITUTE: I'll get you for this.

OLD LADY: What a life, what a life!

WIFE: (TO THE DRUNK) You'll wish you'd never been born!

GERVAISE AND COUPEAU ARRIVE AT THE TOP OF THE TENEMENT. THE LORILLEUXS APPEAR. LORILLEUX WORKS WITH HIS TWEEZERS ON SOME OBJECT BETWEEN HIS FINGERS. MME LORILLEUX SITS AT HER WORKBENCH WHERE SHE PULLS BLACK METAL WIRE WITH PLIERS. THEY WORK IN SILENCE.

COUPEAU: (CALLING) We're here!

MME L: Ah, there you are. We're on a rush order. Come in but stay out of the workroom.

GERVAISE AND COUPEAU ENTER THE APARTMENT.

MME L: (REGISTERING GERVAISE) So this is her, is it?

COUPEAU: That's right.

ANOTHER SILENCE. GERVAISE WHISPERS TO COUPEAU.

GERVAISE: I don't see any gold.

COUPEAU: It's there.

GERVAISE: Where?

COUPEAU: That wire my sister's handling. It comes like that. You have to draw it out. You have to be strong. Skilful too.

LORILLEUX HEARING THIS FINALLY LOOKS UP.

26

LORILLEUX: And I make column-chain.
GERVAISE: Sorry?
COUPEAU: There's small-link, heavy-curb, watch-chain and column. Lorilleux only makes column chain.
LORILLEUX: And you know something? Only today I did a calculation. I started doing this when I was twelve. And you know how long a column I must have made up until today ? (PAUSE) Eight thousand metres. That's nearly enough to go from here to Versailles. Makes you think, eh?

HE LAUGHS. THE LAUGH TURNS TO A COUGH.
GERVAISE IS BAFFLED BUT TRIES TO SMILE. COUPEAU DECIDES TO TAKE THE INITIATIVE.

COUPEAU: We're relying on you, you know, Lorilleux.
LORILLEUX: Oh?
COUPEAU: To be my wife's witness. At the wedding.

LORILLEUX LOOKS UP AND STARES.

LORILLEUX: You mean you're serious?
COUPEAU: Yes, of course.

LORILLEUX LOOKS AT HIS WIFE WHO NOW STUDIES GERVAISE.

MME L: Well, mademoiselle, in my experience marriage doesn't very often work out - even when you can afford it. But, of course, my brother's free to do as he

27

	pleases. It's hardly our affair. Even if you do have two children.
GERVAISE:	(BRIDLING) Yes, what of it?
MME L:	Well, forgive me but she doesn't look very robust, does she, Lorilleux?
GERVAISE:	You mean I'm lame? Well, let me -
COUPEAU:	(CUTTING IN) Look, let's consider the matter settled, shall we? The wedding's on Saturday the 29th. How does that suit?
MME L:	It's up to you. You don't need to ask us. And if it's what you want, Lorilleux will be a witness. You know us, anything for a quiet life.

GERVAISE RISES BRISKLY, EAGER TO GO BEFORE SHE LOSES HER TEMPER.

GERVAISE:	Well, that's settled then.

THEY START TO LEAVE.

LORILLEUX:	Just a moment -

GERVAISE STOPS STARTLED.
HE COMES UP TO HER WITH A
BRUSH.

LORILLEUX:	You see, tiny specks of gold can cling to the soles of your shoes. Just let me check - and you, Coupeau.

HE BRUSHES THE SOLES OF THEIR FEET, HOLDING HIS APRON OUT TO CATCH ANY SPECKS OF GOLD. AS SOON AS HE CAN, COUPEAU GRABS GERVAISE'S HAND.

COUPEAU:	Come on, Gervaise.

HE PULLS HER AWAY. THE
LORILLEUXS LEAVE.

COUPEAU: I'm sorry. They're stingy sods.
GERVAISE: Doesn't say much for our chances of
              happiness, does it?
COUPEAU: Bollocks to them. We're getting married
              on the 29th.

*****

MUSIC. MA COUPEAU ENTERS
WITH A WEDDING DRESS. SHE
HELPS GERVAISE ON WITH IT.
COUPEAU WATCHES HER FONDLY.

COUPEAU: It's cost us all we've got but you only get
              married once. Isn't that right, ma?
MA COUPEAU: That's right, son.
COUPEAU: Looks lovely, doesn't she, ma?
MA COUPEAU: A real treat.
GERVAISE: (APOLOGETICALLY) Belonged to one
              of the boss's laundrywomen who died.
              The husband let me have it cheap.
COUPEAU: (NERVOUSLY) Ready?
GERVAISE: (NODDING) Yes.
MA COUPEAU: God bless you, son, and you, love.

SHE KISSES GERVAISE. MADINIER
ENTERS.

MADINIER: I trust I'm not too early.
COUPEAU: No, glad to see you. Gervaise, Monsieur
              Madinier who lives down from my sister
              and her husband.
MADINIER: My felicitations.

THEY SHAKE HANDS. THE OTHER
GUESTS ARRIVE - MADAME LERAT
AND THE LORILLEUXS.

COUPEAU: My other sister - Madame Lerat.
MME LERAT: (KISSING GERVAISE) The widow,
               love. She who sleeps alone.

THE WEDDING PARTY GROUPS
ITSELF WITH MUCH FUSSING.
RELIGIOUS MUSIC.
THE PRIEST ENTERS.
THE CEREMONY IS A SHORT
DRONE OF INCOMPREHENSIBLE
LATIN.

PRIEST: In nomine patrii et filii et spiritus sancti.
               Et pax vobiscum. Amen.

THE PRIEST LEAVES.
AN AWKWARD SILENCE.

COUPEAU: (TRYING TO JOKE) So that's it then?
               Well, I suppose you can't expect much
               for five francs!
MADINIER: Still makes it a proper marriage, doesn't
               it?

MES-BOTTES RUSHES IN THEN
STOPS IN EMBARRASSMENT.

MES-B: (TO COUPEAU) Oh, have I missed it?
               Sorry, mate.
COUPEAU: You haven't missed much yet. We're only
               just starting to enjoy ourselves.

MA COUPEAU PROMPTLY BURSTS
INTO TEARS.

GERVAISE:	It's alright, ma, I'll make him happy, don't worry. After all, I want to be happy too.
COUPEAU:	So what now? We've got four hours till dinner.
MME LERAT:	Yes, and it looks like rain.
MME L:	Well, I haven't made the effort to look special to stand around on a street corner.
COUPEAU:	There's must be something nice we can do to pass the time. Any ideas, Gervaise?
GERVAISE:	Anything you like. I'm not fussy.
COUPEAU:	(DEFERRING) Monsieur Madinier?
MADINIER:	Well, of course, we could go to the museum.
THE OTHERS:	(VARIOUSLY) The what?
MADINIER:	The museum - the Louvre. There are antiquities there. Drawings, paintings, that sort of thing. It's something you all ought to see at least once in your life.

THE PARTY IS UNCERTAIN HOW
TO REACT AND EVERYONE LOOKS
AT EVERYBODY ELSE.
THEN MES-BOTTES SPEAKS:

MES-B:	Why not?
MME LERAT:	It's seem a nice idea. Very suitable.
MADINIER:	That's agreed then. Follow me.

MUSIC. MADINIER LEADS THE
PARTY CONFIDENTLY OFF. IT IS
RAINING AND THEY HAVE TO PUT
UP UMBRELLAS AND STEP OVER
PUDDLES.
TWO UPPER-CLASS WOMEN PASS
BY AND STARE AT THEM.
THE WEDDING PROCESSION
MOVES ON.

31

MME L: (TO HER HUSBAND) I'm not surprised
                at them staring. Look at her. Peg-Leg.

                NES-BOTTES AT THE BACK OF THE
                PARTY HEARS THIS AND IMITATES
                GERVAISE'S LIMP AS THEY ALL
                HURRY ON.

MES-B: Peg. Leg. Peg, Leg. Peg. Leg.

                FINALLY THE PARTY STOPS.

MADINIER: (GESTURING) Here we are. The
                Louvre.

                HE GESTURES AS IF TOWARDS AN
                IMPOSING BUILDING. THE OTHERS
                LOOK TOWARDS IT OVER-AWED.

GERVAISE: You're sure it's alright for us to go in?
MADINIER: But, of course. It's our heritage.

                THEY ENTER AS IF GOING INTO A
                SPACIOUS AND GRAND HALL.
                AN   IMPOSING   ATTENDANT
                STARES AT THEM.
                THE PARTY GETS MORE SELF-
                CONSCIOUS STILL.

MADINIER: (TAKING CONTROL) Come on, no
                point in all standing here. There's lots for
                us to see!

                HE LEADS THE PARTY ON. THE
                IMPOSING ATTENDANT SEEMS TO
                BE   EVERYWHERE.   MADINIER
                LEADS THEM CONFIDENTLY INTO
                A ROOM. HIS FACE FALLS.

MADINIER: Oh no. Ah, this way.

THEY BACKTRACK AS MADINIER
SEARCHES FOR THE RIGHT WAY.
SUDDENLY THEY APPARENTLY
ENTER A LARGE DARK ROOM.

GERVAISE: (DISTURBED) Where is this?
MADINIER: The Assyrian Gallery. (PAUSE) That's an
               Assyrian goddess over there. Half cat
               half woman. And underneath is an
               inscription in Assyrian.

THEY PEER AT THIS STILL A BIT
SCARED.
COUPEAU BREAKS THE MOOD.

COUPEAU: Who'd ever read scribble like that? I
               could do better myself.

THEY ALL LAUGH IN RELIEF -
APART FROM MADINIER.

MADINIER: Come along, let's not waste time here. It's
               the first floor you really all ought to see.
               The Galleries of French Painting.

ANOTHER MUDDLED TREK AND
THEN SUDDENLY THEY ARE IN
THE PAINTING GALLERIES.
THEY LOOK ABOUT SELF-
CONSCIOUSLY.

COUPEAU: Christ, look at all these pictures! Must be
               worth a fucking fortune.

GERVAISE HUSHES HIM. THEY
MOVE AS A GROUP STARING AT

33

PAINTINGS AS MADINIER CALLS
OUT THEIR NAMES.

MADINIER: The Wedding at Cana ...

THEY STARE UNABLE TO COME UP
WITH ANY REACTION.

MADINIER: Venus and Mars ...

THEY STARE IN AMAZEMENT.

MME LERAT: She's not wearing a thing. And what
you'd see if that gentleman wasn't
holding his shield where it is, I can't
begin to imagine.

MA C: (TO LERAT) You know, Julie, she
reminds me a bit of your Auntie Louise.
She was a big woman like that.

MES-B: Runs in the family, eh?

AGAIN THE SCOWL OF THE
ATTENDANT. THEY MOVE ON.

MADINIER: (CLEARING HIS THROAT) The Mona
Lisa.

THIS TIME THEY'RE GENUINELY
AFFECTED BY WHAT THEY'RE
LOOKING AT.
MUSIC CREEPS IN - A HAUNTING
CHOPIN MELODY.
THEY STAND STILL AND RAPT AS
IF THEY'RE SUSPENDED IN TIME.
THEN THEY BECOME SELF-
CONSCIOUS AGAIN.
THE MUSIC FADES.

34

GERVAISE: It's lovely. Course I don't anything about pictures.
MA C: Me neither. But I know what I like.
COUPEAU: Me, I'd rather have the Venus. More for your money if you know what I mean.

HIS MOTHER AND SISTERS LOOK A BIT DISAPPROVING BUT THE MEN ALL LAUGH AND THE SOLEMN MOOD IS BROKEN.

MADINIER: There's a great deal more to see.
COUPEAU: Gervaise?
GERVAISE: I don't mind really, I ...

THE ATTENDANT CROSSES THE STAGE:

ATTENDANT: Everybody out! The museum's closing!
LORILLEUX: Looks like we've had it anyway.
GERVAISE: Oh well, another time perhaps.
MADINIER: Just so. Now I think there's a quick way out ....

THEY BUNDLE AFTER HIM - A WEARYING STRAGGLING GROUP.
A CLOCK STRIKES FOUR. MME LORILLEUX TURNS TO HER HUSBAND.

MME L: Still two hours to dinner-time.

THEN FESTIVE MUSIC STRIKES UP. GERVAISE AND COUPEAU DANCE A POLKA. THE OTHERS JOIN IN. AS THE DANCING FINISHES AMID CONGRATULATIONS, MADINIER PRODUCES A PLATE.

MADINIER: Come on, ladies and gents, you've had your supper. Now it's time to pay up.

LORILLEUX: These dos where you go dutch never work out, do they? Some always eat more than others. Drink more too.

MME LORILLEUX GLARES AT MES-BOTTES AS HE PUTS HIS MONEY IN.

MME L: I could have done it twice as good for half the price at home. And without some lout pouring chicken gravy all over me. Look.

SHE TURNS TO LORILLEUX.

MME L: Shall we be off, Lorilleux? Leave my brother with Peg Leg.

GERVAISE HEARS THIS BUT DOESN'T RESPOND.

MME L: (TO COUPEAU) You're not sleeping at her place, are you?

COUPEAU: Yeah. And why not? The kids aren't there tonight.

MME L: Well, really, you should at least have put the wedding off until you could have afforded something decent.

COUPEAU: Well, we haven't, have we?

MES-B: (FAIRLY DRUNK) Now, now, all friends here. And God bless the happy couple.

HE GIVES THE RELUCTANT GERVAISE A SLOPPY KISS. THE OTHERS TAKE THEIR FAREWELLS.

36

FINALLY JUST COUPEAU AND
GERVAISE ARE LEFT.
LIGHTS CHANGE. HE KISSES HER
THEN REACHES IN HIS POCKET.

COUPEAU: Seven sous. That's all we've got to start
            married life on.
GERVAISE: Well, we'll just have to work bloody
            hard, won't we? And we'll get our own
            place in the end, I know we will.
COUPEAU: Course.
GERVAISE: And, after that, you know what? I want to
            get my own shop, my own laundry.

A DRUNKEN BAZOUGE LURCHES
PAST THEM AND BOWS.

GERVAISE: Who's this?
COUPEAU: Bazouge. He lives in my sister's block
            too. (SOFTLY) The undertaker's man.

GERVAISE   STARES   AT   THE
LURCHING GRINNING FIGURE.

COUPEAU: He's quite harmless.
BAZOUGE: And as good as the next man, my dear.
            I've had a few I admit. When you're busy,
            you have to grease the wheel. And the
            two of you couldn't have got a stiff
            weighing thirty stone down four flights
            without breaking a single bone now could
            you?

GERVAISE SHUDDERS. BAZOUGE
REGISTERS THIS.

BAZOUGE: Oh, you'll go yourself one day, dear. And
            you could be glad of it. I know a lot of
            women who are.

37

HE BOWS DRUNKENLY AND
TAKES HIS LEAVE.

COUPEAU: Take no notice.

HE LEADS HER AWAY. TENDER
MUSIC. THEY EMBRACE.
COUPEAU LOVINGLY HELPS
GERVAISE OFF WITH HER
WEDDING DRESS AND THEN PUTS
AN APRON ROUND HER WAIST.
IT'S PADDED AND AS SHE
ADVANCES TO JOIN OTHER
LAUNDRESSES AT WORK, IT'S
CLEAR SHE'S NOW PREGNANT.

******

COUPEAU APPEARS UP ON THE
ROOF WORKING.
MEANWHILE GERVAISE STARTS
TO WORK AT THE IRONING
ALONGSIDE ANOTHER
LAUNDRESS.
COUPEAU AND GERVAISE BREAK
OFF THEIR WORK AND TALK
INTIMATELY AS IF AT HOME IN
BED AND HALF-ASLEEP.

COUPEAU: Gervaise -
GERVAISE: Mmm?
COUPEAU: Gervaise -
GERVAISE: Mmm...
COUPEAU: I love you. You know that, don't you?
GERVAISE: I love you too.
COUPEAU: You're alright?
GERVAISE: Yes. I was just thinking...

38

COUPEAU:	About the baby?
GERVAISE:	Mmmm...
COUPEAU:	I wish you'd chuck the laundry in. I'd like to look after you now.
GERVAISE:	No, no, I don't mind working hard for you because you make me very happy. We're going to need every penny we get.
COUPEAU:	You mustn't overdo it, you know.
GERVAISE:	Anyway it's you who should be careful up there on the roof all day. I'll stop when the pains start. (QUIETLY) Boy or girl?
COUPEAU:	A girl maybe. Either'd be nice.

HE CUTS OFF AS HE CALLS OFF TO
HIS ASSISTANT.

COUPEAU:	Oi, Zidore, stop daydreaming, gives us the irons will you?

COUPEAU WORKS.
AN   OLD   WOMAN   WITH
BINOCULARS WATCHES HIM.
GERVAISE CARRIES ON IRONING.
OTHER WOMEN WORK WITH HER.
SUDDENLY   HER   LABOUR   PAINS
START.
SHE TRIES TO CARRY ON BUT THE
PAIN IS TOO MUCH.
THE   OTHER   LAUNDRESS
REGISTERS THIS.

LAUNDRESS:	Are you alright, Gervaise?
GERVAISE:	Fine. I'll just -
LAUNDRESS:	You ought to go home, you know. I'll come with you if you like.
GERVAISE:	(SHAKING HER HEAD) Don't be silly. I'll be fine for a few hours.
LAUNDRESS:	You're sure?

GERVAISE: Maybe just let the midwife in rue de la
               Charbonniere know.

               SHE STARTS TO MOVE ACROSS
               THE STAGE, FIGHTING THE PAIN.
               BUT SHE SUDDENLY COLLAPSES.
               THE OTHER WOMEN GATHER
               AROUND HER.
               SHE GIVES BIRTH.
               THE APRON IS REMOVED AS SHE
               STRUGGLES AND BUNDLED UP TO
               BECOME THE BABY. ALL THE
               WOMEN COO.

LAUNDRESS: It's a girl.
COUPEAU: (STILL ON THE ROOF) Of course, it is.
               I said I wanted a girl so she's given me a
               girl. (JOKINGLY) You give me
               everything I want, don't you, love? Let's
               take a good look at you, shall we? Now I
               hope you're going to grow up to be a
               good little girl and not go running after
               the boys. You're going to be a sensible
               girl like your Mum and Dad, aren't you,
               Nana?

               DURING THIS, NANA HAS
               ENTERED AS A THREE YEAR OLD.
               SHE TAKES THE BABY AS SHE
               SITS, LISTENING TO HER FATHER,
               WHILE HER MOTHER COMBS HER
               HAIR.
               AS COUPEAU FINISHES, NANA
               SMILES.

GERVAISE: (STILL COMBING NANA'S HAIR) I
               had quite a turn today, Coupeau.
COUPEAU: Oh?

GERVAISE: You know that little haberdasher's shop in the block where your sister lives? Well, Nana and I went there to get some thread.

COUPEAU: And?

GERVAISE: Well, you know we've always wanted to live in that building. The shop's to let. And there are three other rooms beside the shop. All quite small but nicely laid out. Anyway, room enough for us now Claude's left home. Pity it's too expensive.

COUPEAU: (DRILY) So you asked the price then?

GERVAISE: Only out of curiosity.

COUPEAU: You want it for your laundry, don't you?

GERVAISE: I've told you, it's too expensive. And well, maybe I wouldn't be any good running my own business.

COUPEAU: Bollocks. If you're set on it, take it. We can get the cash together. If you can stick being in the same building as my sister.

GERVAISE: I've nothing against her. But -

COUPEAU: We'll go together when I've finished work. (PAUSE) You really want it, don't you?

GERVAISE: (NODDING) Yes.

SHE STROKES NANA'S HAIR.
COUPEAU STARES AT THE OLD WOMAN.

COUPEAU: (AS IF TO ZIDORE) What's she looking at? Gives you the creeps her staring like that day after day.

GERVAISE: Come on, Nana, we're going to see daddy at work.

SHE LEADS NANA OFF ROUND THE STAGE WHILE COUPEAU HAILS

41

MADAME BOCHE PASSING WITH SHOPPING.

COUPEAU: Hello there, Madame Boche.

SHE STOPS AND LOOKS UP.

COUPEAU: Everything alright with you?
MME B: Yes, thanks. I'm off to the butcher to get us a nice leg of mutton. How's Gervaise - and little Nana?
COUPEAU: Fine thanks. I'm expecting them any time now. Nana's never seen her daddy at work.
MME B;   Well, I better not keep you.

COUPEAU MOVES AWAY WORKING ON THE ROOF.
BUT THEN GERVAISE APPEARS WITH NANA. MME BOCHE CALLS:

MME B: Gervaise!

BUT GERVAISE GESTURES FOR HER TO BE QUIET.

MME B: What's the matter?
GERVAISE: I don't want him to see me all of a sudden. It's silly, I know, but I'm scared he'll lose his balance.
MME B: Well, I suppose I wouldn't like it if it was my old man up there.
GERVAISE: I used to worry all the time. But I suppose you can get used to anything in time.

BUT SHE STILL LOOKS UP ANXIOUSLY. COUPEAU TURNS,

42

SPOTS THEM AND COMES BACK
ACROSS THE ROOF.

COUPEAU: Creeping up on me, are you? She's scared to call out, you know, Madame Boche. Silly isn't it? I've only got a chimney cowl to fix - I'll be down in no time at all.

HE LOOKS AROUND.

COUPEAU: Zidore? Where's the boy got to? Oi, come back here. These roofs aren't for strolling about on, you know. Pass me the irons.

MME BOCHE, NANA AND
GERVAISE WATCH.
MME BOCHE SPOTS THE OLD
LADY.

MME B: Look at that nosy old cow. What's she waiting for?

COUPEAU: (CALLING DOWN) I'm finished now. And I'm coming down.

HE STARTS TO CLIMB DOWN.
GERVAISE SMILES IN RELIEF AS
HE DESCENDS. THEN NANA CRIES
OUT: Daddy, daddy, look at me!
COUPEAU TURNS TO LOOK AND
SMILES. HE LOSES HIS FOOTING.

COUPEAU: Jesus!

HE FALLS. GERVAISE SCREAMS.
COUPEAU'S BODY ROLLS ACROSS
THE GROUND AND THEN IS STILL.
A CROWD OF PEOPLE GATHERS,
GOUJET AMONG THEM.

MME BOCHE PULLS NANA ASIDE
BUT NANA STILL TRIES TO LOOK.
THE OLD LADY LEAVES,
APPARENTLY SATISFIED.

GOUJET: It's bad. We ought to take him to the
               hospital.
GERVAISE: No, home. Take him home.
MME B: It'll cost a fortune if he's treated at home.
GERVAISE: If he goes to hospital, I know he'll never
               get out alive. He's my husband. I've got
               the money we've saved for the laundry.
               Carry him back home please. Please.

AND THE GROANING COUPEAU IS
CARRIED HOME BY GOUJET.
HE'S LAID OUT ON A MATTRESS
ON THE FLOOR.
MUSIC. GERVAISE WATCH OVER
COUPEAU IN SILENT VIGIL.
LIGHTS CHANGE. COUPEAU IS
STILL IN BED ASLEEP. GERVAISE IS
ALONE WITH HIM. GOUJET COMES
IN.

GERVAISE: Oh come in, Monsieur Goujet
GOUJET: How is he?
GERVAISE: It's been a difficult couple of weeks but
               he's out of danger now, the doctor says.
GOUJET: Thanks to you.

GERVAISE   JUST   SHRUGS,
EMBARRASSED   AT   THE
INTENSITY.

GOUJET: Is there anything I can do?
GERVAISE: You and your mother have done enough.
               You've been very kind. And I should be

able to catch up on the housework now he's on the mend. Do sit down, please.

GOUJET SITS AND WATCHES HER.

COUPEAU: Who's there?

GERVAISE: Monsieur Goujet. The foundryman from opposite.

COUPEAU: (NOT VERY INTERESTED) Oh.

GOUJET: I never doubted you'd get better, Monsieur Coupeau. Your wife, well, she's been wonderful.

COUPEAU: (TURNING AWAY) I know.

GERVAISE: Your mother was telling me you're soon naming the day soon yourself, Monsieur Goujet.

GOUJET: Yes. She's a lacemaker like my mum. She's a very nice girl. We've got money put away and we're supposed to be getting married in September.

GERVAISE: Supposed?

GOUJET: Not all women are like you, Madame Coupeau.

GOUJET LAPSES BACK INTO EMBARRASSED SILENCE.
THE LORILLEUXS ENTER.

MME L: I don't suppose he's any better but we thought we'd come anyway. He'd have been back on his feet in half the time if you'd let him go into hospital.

GERVAISE: He'd have hated it.

LORILLEUX: If you count the doctor and the medicines and the food and the pay you've both lost, you must be eating into your savings. Time's money.

MME L:	When Lorilleux was ill, he went straight into hospital so if you get into difficulties, don't look to us for any help.
GERVAISE:	We're managing fine, thanks.

SHE ATTENDS TO COUPEAU.

MME L:	And what about the shop then? When are you taking that?
LORIELLUX:	That's right. Only yesterday the concierge was asking when to expect you.

GERVAISE IS UPSET. GOUJET REGISTERS THIS AS HE'S ABOUT TO LEAVE.

GERVAISE:	I'll be along once Coupeau's on his feet. Tell the concierge that.
MME L:	Alright, we'll tell her. (POINTEDLY) Monsieur Goujet.
LORILLEUX:	Monsieur Goujet.

THEY EXCHANGE A KNOWING LOOK. THEY AND GOUJET LEAVE SEPARATELY.
COUPEAU IS ALONE. MA COUPEAU COMES IN TO SEE HIM.

MA C:	How are you, son?
COUPEAU:	Jesus, I'm sick of this fucking leg, ma. Two months staring up at the ceiling. I know the cracks so well, I could draw them from memory. I'm like an old man. There's no justice in this world, ma.
MA C:	(DISTRESSED) Son... son...
COUPEAU:	Dad fell and broke his neck when he was pissed. He deserved it. I was stone cold sober, not a drop of booze in me, and all I did, all I did, was to turn round to smile

46

at Nana. And - (HE BREAKS OFF) If there's a God up there, I don't know what the fuck he thinks he's doing.

GERVAISE RETURNS AS MA COUPEAU LEAVES GIVING HER A SHRUG OF DESPAIR.
ALONE AGAIN WITH COUPEAU, GERVAISE GIVES HIM HIS CRUTCHES. HE LEARNS TO USE THEM DURING:

COUPEAU: It's a lousy job anyway. If I had my way I'd send every bugger who wants his roof fixed up there to fix it himself. It's a mug's game. Why didn't I learn something cushier - like cabinet-making or something. Out in all weathers risking life and limb and for what?

HE LOSES PATIENCE WITH THE CRUTCHES.

COUPEAU: Fuck these bloody things. (HE SITS SELF-PITYINGLY) I'm never going to be able to go up there again. I couldn't if I wanted to. But what am I going to do? I can't just sit around for ever.

GERVAISE: Stop tormenting yourself, Coupeau. It'll all take time. There's no rush. (PULLING OUT A COIN) Look, I got paid yesterday. Go out and give yourself a treat. I've got to get to the laundry.

HE TAKES THE MONEY AND SLUMPS IN A CHAIR.
GERVAISE HURRIES OFF.

COUPEAU: (CALLING AFTER HER) All my life I've worked my bollocks off. I deserve a break.

GERVAISE IS COMING BACK FROM WORK AT THE LAUNDRY WITH CLEMENCE.

CLEMENCE: Are you alright, Gervaise? You've been looking knackered all day.
GERVAISE: I'm fine, Clemence.
CLEMENCE: Can't you get that husband of yours back to work?
GERVAISE: He needs to rest.
CLEMENCE: What, for four months? All those mouths to feed and you're the only one working. Must be tough.
GERVAISE: (TIGHTLY) We manage, thank you. (PAUSE) And Coupeau'll go back to work when he's good and ready, you'll see.
CLEMENCE: (SCEPTICALLY) Course.

GERVAISE RETURNS HOME. COUPEAU IS BEATING ETIENNE. ETIENNE RUNS CRYING INTO HER ARMS. COUPEAU STAGGERS, A BIT DRUNK, LIMPING.

GERVAISE: What's happening?
COUPEAU: Fucking brat, giving me lip.

HE APPROACHES ETIENNE WHO RUNS AWAY. HE RUNS TO GOUJET WHO'S ABOUT TO CALL BUT NOW STANDS COMFORTING ETIENNE UNCERTAIN WHAT TO DO.

48

COUPEAU:	Not as if he's my child, is it? I'm a sick man. And I'm entitled to respect. I'm the master of this house.
GERVAISE:	But you've always got along fine. What's he done?
COUPEAU:	It doesn't matter what he's done. He's not showing me proper respect, that's all.
GERVAISE:	Did you go out?
COUPEAU:	Yes, I had a drink if you must know - with the lads. Don't worry, just a glass of wine, that's all. But a drink now and then never killed anybody, did it? And then I went and saw my sister. Wanted to know when you were starting your shop.
GERVAISE:	(QUIETLY) Well, that's not going to be for a long time, is it now? Not with all our savings gone. It'll take years to -
COUPEAU:	Don't start on that for God's sake.
GERVAISE:	Coupeau -
COUPEAU:	Just don't start, alright?

HE STOMPS AWAY PAST GOUJET.
GERVAISE FOLLOWS HIM.
THEN STOPS WHEN SHE SEES
GOUJET STANDING THERE.

GOUJET:	Madame Coupeau - will you let me lend you the money?
GERVAISE:	Money? What for?
GOUJET:	For your shop.
GERVAISE:	Look, I couldn't possibly take money from you.
GOUJET:	It's only a loan. I know you'd make a success of the shop.
GERVAISE:	I can't. I mean, isn't the money put aside for your marriage?

GOUJET:	No, I've - I've given up the idea. I'd much rather lend you the money.
GERVAISE:	But what does your mother say?
GOUJET:	She wants to speak to you.

MUSIC. MADAME GOUJET, A DARK, GLOOMY FIGURE, ENTERS AND SITS.

GOUJET:	Mother, I've told her I want to give her the money.
MME GOUJET:	Madame Gervaise, you know how fond I am of you. You're a hard-working woman, the laundry's a good idea, but I'm afraid I don't hold out any hope for its success.
GOUJET:	Mother -
MME GOUJET:	I'm sorry but it's your husband. He's going to the bad as fast as he can.
GERVAISE:	He's a sick man.
MME GOUJET:	He'll squander every penny you make, Madame Gervaise.
GOUJET:	Mother, please -
GERVAISE:	Alright, you don't want me to have the money. You've both been quite generous enough.
MME GOUJET:	My son wants to give you the money. He's a good boy and if that's what he wants, then that's what he shall have. (PAUSE) What exactly is the sum you need?
GERVAISE:	Well, I'm afraid, for the rent, for fitting out the place, and something to live on for the first few weeks till things get going, it's going to take at least five hundred francs. But -
MME GOUJET:	Then five hundred francs it shall be. You can pay us back in monthly instalments of twenty francs.
GOUJET:	Or maybe, mother, she could pay part of it in kind - do the laundry for us.
MME GOUJET:	(WITH A SIGH) If you wish.

GERVAISE STANDS STUNNED. THEN
THE GOUJETS SMILE AND SHE SHAKES
THEM WARMLY BY THE HAND. MME
GOUJET LOOKS ALMOST PITYINGLY AT
HER OVERJOYED SON.

****

IMMEDIATELY   THE   CHATTERING
VOICES OF THE TENEMENT START.
AS   THEY   TALK,   THEY   CREATE
GERVAISE'S LAUNDRY ON THE STAGE.

Have you heard? - someone's taking over the
haberdasher's.
God, there's one born every minute.
Yeah, Marescot's found another mug.
But it's filthy that fucking hole.
You wouldn't catch me going in there.
Me neither - so who's the mug then?
You know Madame Lorilleux up the top?
Wish I didn't.
It's her brother and his wife.
Not Gervaise?
That's the one. She hasn't got a hope, has she?
She certainly hasn't, God help her.
There's one born every minute.

THEY BURST INTO A MOCKING SONG
AS GERVAISE ENTERS AND STARTS TO
MOVE PROUDLY AROUND HER NEW
PREMISES:

There's one born every minute
Who does she think she is?
She hasn't got a bleeding clue
Of how to run a bus - iness.

51

Can't she see? Can't she hear?
Place goes bust - once a year.
When this one has to go -
We can say - I told you so.

THE CHORUS LEAVES. LIGHTS CHANGE.
GERVAISE IS SHOWING MADAME
BOCHE ROUND.

GERVAISE: Well, here it is.
MME B: It's certainly got possibilities.
GERVAISE: (EXCITEDLY) That's it. You see, I'm going to
              have a sign outside painted pale blue saying:
              LAUNDRY: FINEST QUALITY WORK in
              gilt lettering. And there'll be little muslin
              curtains on the window in a blue and white
              stripe.
MME B: Oh, very nice.
GERVAISE: That'll match this wallpaper, you see. And this
              is the big worktable. I've found a lovely piece
              of cretonne to put over it to hide the trestles.
              And I've had a cast-iron stove put in. One that
              can heat ten irons at least.
MME B: That'll keep you busy.
GERVAISE: I'm getting three assistants in.
MME B: (SLIGHTLY ACID) Are you now?

AND AS THE LIGHTS FADE ON
GERVAISE SILENTLY EXPLAINING THE
REST OF HER PLANS, THEY COME UP ON
MADAME LORILLEUX AND HER
HUSBAND.

MME L: She slept with that Goujet to get the money.
              Just imagine Peg Leg running a shop. Whatever
              next?

THE VOICES OF THE TENEMENT TAKE
UP THE GOSSIP:

52

Whatever next?

The airs she's giving herself -

Have you seen the fancy fabrics she's bought?

It's just a laundry, after all, not some tart's boudoir.

That's right. And everyone knows how she got the money.

Who the fuck does she think she is?

I mean, I don't mind people bettering themselves -

But there are limits.

That's right.

And this Peg Leg's way beyond them.

Fine Quality Work indeed!

What about the Fine Quality Work she did to get the money?

She's borrowed up to the hilt.

And spent up to the hilt too.

Well, I give it a couple of months.

Me too - at the most.

Who the fuck does she think she is?

LIGHTS UP AS GERVAISE ENTERS WITH PILES OF DIRTY LAUNDRY - AND HER ASSISTANTS, CLEMENCE, MADAME PUTOIS - AND CLOTHILDE, AN EAGER BUT CLUMSY SIMPLETON.
THEY ARE FEELING THE HEAT. PUTOIS AND FRANCOISE ARE IRONING.
GERVAISE BRINGS A BIG BASKET OF WASHING FOR THEM TO IRON.

GERVAISE: This is your basket, Madame Putois. Try and do it as quickly as you can. In this heat, it'll dry up in no time at all. And Clothilde, do get on with that collar.

CLEMENCE: (SORTING DIRTY LAUNDRY) God, get a

53

GERVAISE: load of the smell of this lot.
Well, they wouldn't send them to us if they weren't dirty now, would they?

SHE GETS DOWN AMONG THE WASHING WITH CLEMENCE.

GERVAISE: Besides, they tell you things. See that pillowcase. That's the Boches. Her hair-oil gets everywhere.

CLEMENCE: What about old Mademoiselle Remanjou's chemises then?

GERVAISE: Well, they always wear out at the top, don't they? She must have the sharpest shoulder blades in Paris. (THE OTHERS LAUGH) But her stuff never gets dirty - I suppose when you're that old and dried up, there's nothing left to drip out of your body.

CLEMENCE OPENS ANOTHER PILE OF WASHING.

CLEMENCE: Oh, Jesus. This is too much.

GERVAISE: Madame Gaudron's ?

CLEMENCE: (NODDING) I mean, I'm not fussy but smell that. It makes you want to puke. She must have been wearing it for months.

GERVAISE: No one else will touch her stuff.

CLEMENCE: No wonder. How's it possible to get your clothes that filthy?

GERVAISE: (SHRUGS) God knows. Still, it's only human, isn't it?

THE WOMEN CONTINUE WORK. IN THE HEAT CLEMENCE PULLS DOWN HER BODICE MUCH TO MADAME PUTOIS'S DISGUST.

PUTOIS: Put your bodice back on, Clemence. Honestly!
                Really, why don't you take everything off while
                you're at it?

                COUPEAU   COMES   IN.   HE'S   BEEN
                DRINKING.

COUPEAU: The heat knocks you out, doesn't it?
GERVAISE: How's the job?
COUPEAU: We knocked off at lunchtime. Went for a
                farewell drink with Coudeloup - he's going
                back to Toulouse. Well, a few drinks then.
                We'd have been alright if it hadn't been for the
                sun. Everybody's flaked out out there.
CLEMENCE: So it's not the booze, it's the sun.

                SHE LAUGHS. COUPEAU GRINS AT HER,
                THEN AT GERVAISE.

GERVAISE: You do talk some rubbish. Why don't you take
                a nap? We're busy and you'll get under our feet.
COUPEAU: (STAGGERING   THROUGH   THE
                WASHING) Give us a kiss.
GERVAISE: Not now, Coupeau.
COUPEAU: Just a little kiss.
CLEMENCE: (STIRRING) Go on, give him a kiss, madame.
                Not often you see an affectionate husband is it?
MME PUTOIS: Wish mine was
GERVAISE: (SIGHING) Oh, alright, then.

                COUPEAU COMES OVER. SHE OFFERS
                HER CHEEK.
                BUT COUPEAU GRABS HOLD OF HER.

COUPEAU: You stink of your dirty washing, my dear. But I
                still love you.
GERVAISE: (GIGGLING) Don't be silly, Coupeau.

                                55

BUT SHE LETS HIM HOLD HER. THE
OTHERS SMIRK.

GERVAISE: Now, be off with you.

SHE PUSHES HIM OFF BUT HE STANDS
SWAYING.

COUPEAU: (SENTIMENTAL) I'm dead worried about my
              mum, Gervaise. Her legs aren't too good and
              she's had to give up her cleaning job. She's not
              going to be able to look after herself much
              longer.
GERVAISE: Well, you'll have to muck in to help her, you
              and your sisters, won't you?
COUPEAU: But they haven't got the money. We haven't got
              the money. And she'll starve, my poor mum'll
              starve.
GERVAISE: Oh, for God's sake, Coupeau, if the worst
              comes to the worst, we'll take her in. Alright?
              Now go and sleep.

COUPEAU STARTS TO LEAVE BUT THEN
LURCHES TOWARDS CLEMENCE AND
STARTS TO FEEL HER UP. CLOTHILDE IS
MESMERISED BY THE SIGHT.

CLEMENCE: I can't work if you do that now, can I?
GERVAISE: (CALMLY) Leave her alone and behave
              yourself.
COUPEAU: I'm just watching, aren't I? Admiring God's
              handiwork. You know, Clemence, with tits like
              that, you could charge to see 'em and nobody'd
              complain.
CLEMENCE: (HALF LAUGHING) Give over.
GERVAISE: Coupeau, come and lie down, will you?
COUPEAU: Can't Clemence come too?
GERVAISE: No, she can't. Now lean on me and we'll get
              you to bed.

56

COUPEAU: But I'm not sleepy.

SHE LEADS HIM AWAY UPSTAGE.
CLEMENCE BURSTS INTO GIGGLES.
CLOTHILDE LOOKS BEWILDERED.

CLEMENCE: The randy sod! The silly randy sod!

BUT GERVAISE RETURNS AND
CLEMENCE HIDES HER LAUGHTER.

GERVAISE: Don't take any notice of him, Clemence. He's always like that when he's had a few. There's no point in getting angry with him. Men are all the same. It doesn't mean anything. At least he always comes straight home - not like some of them. He loves me, you see - and he's working too now when he feels up to it. You've got to understand, he's had a hard time. He's had a terrible accident and he needs time to get over it. (PAUSE) You understand, don't you?

CLEMENCE: (DRILY) Of course, madame.

SHE AND PUTOIS LOOK SCEPTICALLY AT GERVAISE. THEY ALL RETURN TO WORK. THE LAUNDRESSES REMAIN THERE HALF-LIT THROUGHOUT THE FOLLOWING SECTION.

****

THE STAGE FILLS WITH THE SOUNDS OF THE FOUNDRY WITH THE FOUNDRYMEN HALF-SEEN AMONGST THE BILLOWING SMOKE AND THE RED GLOW OF THE FIRES.
GERVAISE APPEARS WITH HER BASKET.
BEC-SALE PASSES.

GERVAISE:	Excuse me - (BEC-SALE TURNS) A boy works here - his name's Etienne - he's my son.
BEC-SALE:	(SHAKING HIS HEAD) Search me, love.
GERVAISE:	Monsieur Goujet then - you know him. He got my son the job.
BEC-SALE:	Oh yeah, Goujet, of course. (HE GRINS) This way, my love.

HE CALLS FOR GOUJET. THE SOUNDS OF THE FOUNDRY DECREASE AND GOUJET AND HIS FELLOW-WORKERS BECOME MORE VISIBLE.
GOUJET LOOKS UP AS GERVAISE APPROACHES HESITANTLY.
THE OTHER MEN STOP TO APPRAISE THE NEW ARRIVAL.

GOUJET:	(DELIGHTED) Why, Madame Gervaise -
GERVAISE:	I've been meaning to come for ages and see where Etienne works. But with all this (SHE INDICATES LAUNDRY) I've not got round to it.
GOUJET:	Don't worry, please. I'm glad you're here at last.

GOUJET RECOMMENCES WORK AT HIS ANVIL BEATING THE REDHOT METAL INTO RIVETS. GERVAISE WATCHES FASCINATED.

GOUJET:	(EXPLAINING AS HE WORKS) These are twenty millimetre rivets I'm turning out. You can do up to three hundred in a day.

HE CONTINUES TO WORK. BEC-SALE RETURNS AND SIDLES UP TO GERVAISE.

BEC-SALE:	(TOO CLOSE) Getting along OK, my love?
GERVAISE:	Yes, thanks.

BEC-SALE:	You're Coupeau's missus aren't you? The penny's just dropped. The name's Bec-Salé.
GERVAISE:	You know my husband?
BEC-SALE:	Had a drink with him only yesterday. Good bloke Coupeau.

GOUJET REALISING HE'S GETTING FRESH GETS ANGRY.

GOUJET:	Listen, we're supposed to finish those forty-millimetres today.
BEC-SALE:	Any time, mate.
GOUJET:	If you're not sneaking back to the boozer that is.
BEC-SALE:	(TO GERVAISE) Look at him, the big baby, talking tough. And just forget about those muscles of his. I can wipe the floor with him at this job any day.
GOUJET:	Then come and do it then. Now.

A BRIEF CONFRONTATIONAL PAUSE.
THE OTHER MEN BECOME ONLOOKERS.

BEC-SALE:	Right, you're on, smart-arse. (TURNING TO GERVAISE) And the little lady will judge which of us does the better job, eh, love?

GERVAISE CAUGHT BETWEEN EXCITEMENT AND A SENSE OF THE ABSURDITY OF THE CONTEST CAN ONLY NOD.

GOUJET:	Let's get started.
BEC-SALE:	The forty millimetres it is. I'll strike first.
GOUJET:	Right.

A RED HOT PIECE OF METAL IS PLACED ON THE ANVIL WITH TONGS.

WORKER 1:   Ready? start!

BEC-SALE HAMMERS THE METAL
FRENETICALLY, THE RHYTHM JAGGED
AND FORCED. HE FINISHES TOO
QUICKLY AND DISPLAYS THE RIVET
HE'S MADE WITH TRIUMPH.

BEC-SALE: There.
WORKER 2:   (EXAMINING IT) It's bent to buggery, Bec-
                Salé
BEC-SALE: (BREATHING HEAVILY) Bollocks.
                (HOLDING IT CLOSE TO GERVAISE)
                Lovely piece of work, isn't it, darling?
GERVAISE: I'm sorry, I can't say.
BEC-SALE: (PEEVED) Right, your turn, smartarse!

MUSIC. GOUJET BEGINS TO BEAT THE
METAL IN A SLOW, POWERFUL
RHYTHM.
AS HE CONTINUES TO HAMMER, AS IF
SUSPENDED IN TIME, GERVAISE
WATCHES HIM FASCINATED AND
AROUSED.
THE MOMENT IS BROKEN AS GOUJET
MAKES HIS FINAL STROKE.
SHE EXAMINES THE FINISHED RIVET.

GERVAISE: It's perfect.
WORKER: The winner!
BEC-SALE: (SOURLY) Alright, don't go on. It was only a
                joke.

HE WALKS AWAY WITH THE OTHER
WORKERS.
THE DIN RECEDES. GOUJET IS ALONE
WITH GERVAISE.
THERE'S AN AWKWARD SILENCE NOW.

60

GERVAISE: I'd never imagined it was like that.
GOUJET: (SHYLY) There's more to see if you like. Like that machine.

WE HEAR THE RUMBLE OF A HUGE RIVET-MAKING MACHINE.
THEY STARE OUT AT IT.

GOUJET: (SUDDENLY) Sometimes I'd like to take my hammer and smash it.
GERVAISE: Whatever for?
GOUJET: That machine can turn out rivets like sausages. Kilogrammes of them in a day. They've cut our wages already. And more cuts on the way. Soon they won't need us at all. Except to feed that machine. (PAUSE) Look - you've got to believe it will be for the good of mankind in the end.
GERVAISE: But they're too regular. I like yours better. You can see yours was made by an artist.

GOUJET SMILES, PLEASED AT THIS.
ANOTHER SILENCE,
THEN GERVAISE INDICATES HER LAUNDRY BASKET.

GERVAISE: I'm sorry but I've got to go now. Thank you for all you're doing for Etienne.
GOUJET: I'll visit you soon, Madame Gervaise.
GERVAISE: Please do, Monsieur Goujet.

SHE WALKS AWAY. GOUJET WATCHES HER GO.
THE LIGHTS FADE ON HIM.
MADAME GOUJET APPEARS.
GERVAISE APPROACHES HER CARRYING THE LAUNDRY BASKET.

MME G: You've brought it all?

61

GERVAISE: Yes, I've not forgotten anything.
MME G: No, that's not one of your faults.

SHE PICKS THROUGH THE LAUNDRY.

GERVAISE: I don't let the girls near your laundry, Madame
                Goujet. I do it myself and I'd go over it ten
                times if necessary. Because it's for you and all
                you've done for me.
MME G: Let's see the list.

SHE STARTS TO CHECK IT. GERVAISE
PLUCKS UP HER COURAGE.

GERVAISE: Madame Goujet, if you don't mind, can I take
                the money for the washing this month? I'm a bit
                pushed.
MME G: (SIGHS) I thought doing our laundry was
                supposed to be a way of clearing the debt
                quicker.
GERVAISE: Just this once. You see, the ten francs will settle
                the stuff I've got on tick from the coal
                merchant.
MME G: Yes, yes, but we've had to go without since my
                son had his wages cut. Maybe you need to do
                the same, not try and get everything on credit
                all the time.
GERVAISE: Coupeau's working again now.
MME G: Now and then I think you mean. (MORE
                GENTLE) You'll soon have nothing left. When
                you're not wise in your youth, you suffer for it
                when you're old.

SHE HANDS GERVAISE THE MONEY.

GERVAISE: Thank you, Madame Goujet. It'll be back to
                normal next month.
MME G: I hope so.

GERVAISE LEAVES. MME GOUJET
WATCHES HER GO.
GERVAISE CARRIES HER LIGHTENED
BASKET OUT INTO THE STREET.
A WOMAN PASSES GERVAISE IN THE
STREET. SHE BUMPS INTO HER AND
PASSES ON.
BUT THEN SOMETHING MAKES HER
STOP AND LOOK BACK.
GERVAISE LOOKS BACK TOO AND
RECOGNISES HER. IT'S VIRGINIE.

VIRGINIE: I don't believe it. Gervaise!
GERVAISE: Virginie!

A SLIGHT AWKWARD PAUSE.

VIRGINIE: So what are you doing her?
GERVAISE: Delivering laundry to Madame Goujet just up
              the road.
VIRGINIE: We live just opposite her now. As of two weeks
              ago.
GERVAISE: Fancy that. I used to live there. (PAUSE) So
              who's 'we'?
VIRGINIE: Me and my old man. I'm a married lady now,
              you know. Nearly coming up to our first
              anniversary.
GERVAISE: Congratulations.
VIRGINIE: Well, I can't grumble. Poisson's a policeman -
              but a decent bloke for all that. There's mackerel
              in here for him. He loves mackerel. And you
              have to spoil a man, don't you? They're like
              babies. (PAUSE) How about you?
GERVAISE: Oh, I'm married too. Remember Coupeau?
VIRGINIE: The tiler?
GERVAISE: That's my husband.
VIRGINIE   Well, well, Madame Coupeau.
GERVAISE: Madame Poisson. (PAUSE) I've got a little girl
              too.

63

VIRGINIE:	Doesn't time fly? (PAUSE) You don't bear any grudge I hope.
GERVAISE:	(SHAKES HEAD) And I hope you don't either. You must drop in and see the shop some time. I've my own laundry.
VIRGINIE:	Well, who'd have thought it? Good for you. I'd love to. We can have a nice chat then when we've more time.
GERVAISE:	I'll look forward to that. Rue de la Goutte d'Or. You can't miss it.

SHE MOVES ON. VIRGINIE WATCHES
HER GO WITH MIXED FEELINGS.
GERVAISE WEARIER NOW ARRIVES AT
THE LORILLEUXS.
THEY'RE AS USUAL HARD AT WORK.

GERVAISE:	I've come to have a word.
MME L:	(NOT LOOKING UP) Oh, yes.
GERVAISE:	Coupeau won't discuss it with you directly so I said I'd come. It's about Ma Coupeau.
MME L:	What about her?
GERVAISE:	She's sixty seven. She's had to give up her last charring job and she's not likely to get another. We can't just leave her to starve, can we?
LORILLEUX:	What are you talking about - starving? She had a good blow-out here only the day before yesterday, didn't she? She's always crying poverty.
GERVAISE:	But we should do something. She's an old woman and there are the three of you who could muck in.

THE   LORILLEUXS   EXCHANGE
GLANCES.

MME L;	Well, I suppose if everybody chipped in, we'd give our five francs.
GERVAISE:	Fifteen francs doesn't get you much.

LORILLEIX: Look, just because there's gold here doesn't
                 mean we're made of money. And she doesn't
                 stint herself you know. She has a drop of spirits
                 when she likes and fresh coffee every morning
                 - every morning. It'd be easy for her to tighten
                 her belt if she wanted to.
GERVAISE: She deserves a few little luxuries at her age,
                 doesn't she?
MME L: Not at our expense, she doesn't. She can see
                 well enough when it comes to getting meat off
                 the bone. No, five francs it is, I'm afraid.

                 LORILLEUX   NODS   AGREEMENT.
                 GERVAISE   HAS   BEEN   GETTING
                 INCREASINGLY ANGRY.

GERVAISE: Alright, if that's the way you want it, keep your
                 bloody money. I'll take in Ma Coupeau. I'd do
                 as much for a stray cat, let alone my husband's
                 mother. And what's more she'll want for
                 nothing, least of all for her morning coffee. So
                 go and get yourself stuffed, you miserable sods.
MME L: (RISING) Don't you dare talk to me like that!
                 And don't count on the five francs either. You
                 can tell her that if she goes to you, I won't even
                 send her a glass of water. Not even if she's
                 dying. Now, get out.
GERVAISE: You know something, you're a bloody monster.

                 SHE TURNS AND LEAVES. TOO LATE
                 LORILLEUX   REALISES   AND   RUNS
                 AFTER HER CALLING: Shoes ! BUT SHE'S
                 ALREADY GONE AND HE RETURNS TO
                 HIS SEAT IN DISGUST.

                 LIGHTS CHANGE. COUPEAU APPEARS
                 WITH MES-BOTTES AND BIBI.
                 HE JOINS THEM IN ANOTHER REPRISE
                 OF: 'Let's go to another bar...'

                 65

LIGHTS. THE LAUNDRY. IT'S COLD NOW AND GERVAISE IS JOINING CLEMENCE AND MADAME PUTOIS IN A CUP OF COFFEE.

CLEMENCE: I'll say one thing for working here. You make a good strong cup of coffee. It was like rats' piss at Madame Fauconnier's.

GERVAISE: You need a treat when you're working this hard. I don't know though, you work hard and where does it get you? The debts seem to get bigger not smaller. I wouldn't mind if I was living it up and having a good time.

PUTOIS: (SHARPLY) Monsieur Coupeau in today?

GERVAISE: (EMBARRASSED) No. He's - he's out. Working I expect.

PUTOIS: Yes, I expect so.

VIRGINIE ENTERS. CLEMENCE LOOKS UP AND SEES HER FIRST.

CLEMENCE: You've got a visitor.

VIRGINIE: It's freezing out there.

GERVAISE: Come on in. This is Clemence - and Madame Putois.

THEY NOD HELLO. VIRGINIE'S EYES TAKE IN THE SHOP.

VIRGINIE: So this is it, is it? My, you have done well for yourself.

GERVAISE: Have a coffee - Madame Poisson.

VIRGINIE: Thanks very much - Madame Coupeau.

THEY BOTH GIGGLE SLIGHTLY.
GERVAISE POURS COFFEE.
CLEMENCE AND PUTOIS RETURN
TO WORK.

GERVAISE It's alright, we're old friends.

VIRGINIE: Well, not always friends perhaps. (SOFTLY) But we've forgotten about the washhouse haven't we?

GERVAISE: (CONSCIOUS OF THE OTHERS' CURIOSITY) Yes, of course.

VIRGINIE: After all, you had every excuse. If it'd have been me, I'd have used a knife. Not that it's brought Lantier and Adele any luck, either of them.

GERVAISE HAS TENSED,
DREADING WHAT'S COMING.

GERVAISE: (VERY SOFT) Oh?

VIRGINIE: No, they went to live in La Glaciere and right from the start they were knocking the living daylights out of each other. But maybe you know that? I've kept in touch of course because in spite of it all, the silly bitch is my sister.

GERVAISE: (SHAKES HEAD) I've not heard hide nor hair of him for - for seven years.

VIRGINIE: (LOOKING ROUND) And look how much better off you are.

GERVAISE: And is he - are they - still living in La Glaciere?

VIRGINIE: Well, they were till a couple of weeks ago.

GERVAISE: What happened then?

VIRGINIE: Adele packed her bags and left.

GERVAISE: (LOUDER) So they're not together any more?

CLEMENCE: (OVER-HEARING) Who isn't?

67

VIRGINIE: (QUICKLY) Nobody you'd know.

                 SHE TALKS MORE SOFTLY TO
                 GERVAISE.

VIRGINIE: What'd you do if he came round now?
GERVAISE: Lantier? I'd send him away with a flea in
                 his ear. I've got my self-respect.
VIRGINIE: Good for you.
GERVAISE: Of course, Etienne's his. And if Lantier
                 wanted to see him, I'd send him over
                 because it's wrong to stop a boy loving
                 his father. And -
CLEMENCE: Whose father's that then?

                 GERVAISE'S VOICE FADES AWAY
                 AT THIS.

GERVAISE: (RISING) I'd better get back to work.
                 We've a lot to do today.
VIRGINIE: (ALSO RISING) Of course. And
                 Poisson'll be thinking I've frozen to death
                 on the way home.

                 BUT AS SHE LEAVES, MA
                 COUPEAU APPEARS CARRYING
                 HER FEW SCRAPS OF BELONGINGS.

MA C: Hello there, Gervaise.
GERVAISE: Hello, ma.
MA C: Did you mean what you said?
GERVAISE: Of course.
MA C: (STARTING TO CRY) Thank God for
                 that. You're a treasure.

                 THE LIGHTS FADE.

THE CHORUS APPEAR SINGING
CARRYING CHAIRS WHICH THEY
SET. WHILE GERVAISE COMFORTS
MA COUPEAU, THEY LAUNCH
INTO AN OFFENBACH-LIKE SONG
OF MOCKERY:

Rising early in the morning,
Hard at work 'till late at night,
Never tiring, never yawning,
Always cheerful, always bright,
Kindly words for everybody,
With a warm and friendly smile -
And a good strong cup of coffee
Makes you feel you're worth a pile.

(CHORUS:)
Oh, what a treasure, oh what a saint,
Works hard all day without complaint,
Oh, what a treasure, oh what a pearl,
What a shining example of a working
girl.

THE CHORUS IS REPEATED. THEN
THE CHORUS LEAVE AS:

****

MA COUPEAU AND GERVAISE LAY
THE TABLE FOR A SUPPER PARTY.

MA C:	Get a whiff of that goose.
GERVAISE:	Doesn't it just?
MA C:	You know, I think that bird's the biggest goose I've ever seen.
GERVAISE:	Well, I wanted something special.
MA C:	You deserve it. You work hard enough. And I'll tell you one thing. I wouldn't be

69

	eating like this if I'd gone to live with that bitch of a daughter of mine.
GERVAISE:	No, not those napkins there, ma. We'll use the damask ones. Especially for the two of them.
MA C:	(CACKLING) That'll really put them off their dinner.
GERVAISE:	Serves them right.
MA C:	(GLEEFULLY) They'll die of envy. You know, I've only seen my five francs twice in all these months.
GERVAISE:	Yes, always some excuse or other.
MA C:	(DISTRACTED) Oh, those smells, Gervaise, they're making me come over all queer. (SMELLING) The bacon with peas...
GERVAISE:	(SMELLING) The blanquette of veal ...
MA C:	The dumplings ...
GERVAISE:	The stew...
MA C:	The chine of pork. The roast potatoes.
GERVAISE:	And the goose.
MA C:	You know something, Gervaise? When she arrives with that husband of hers, I'm going to stand opposite the door and see the look of misery on their faces.
GERVAISE:	(LAUGHING) You do that, ma.

SHE STEPS BACK TO ADMIRE THEIR HANDIWORK.

GERVAISE:	You know, I almost wish we could set the table up outside so that everyone could see. (PAUSE) I keep thinking - we've made it, ma, haven't we, Coupeau and I? Well, nearly anyway.
MA C:	(KISSING HER) Happy saint's day.
GERVAISE:	Thanks, ma.

THE GUESTS START TO ARRIVE.
FIRST COMES VIRGINIE WITH HER
HUSBAND, POISSON. VIRGINIE
GIVES GERVAISE FLOWERS AND
THE WOMEN EMBRACE.

VIRGINIE: This is my husband. Poisson - Madame Coupeau.

POISSON: (BOWING STIFFLY) I'm pleased to make your acquaintance, madame.

VIRGINIE: Wonderful smells. You know, it seems a pity you've been working away at all this food for the last three days and we're going to clear it up in no time. Can't I help at all?

GERVAISE: No, everything's ready. There's only the soup. So make yourself at home.

VIRGINIE: (QUIETLY) I actually saw him the other day, you know, Lantier. Maybe he'll drop in.

GERVAISE SHAKES HER HEAD
QUICKLY. MME LERAT COMES IN
AS POISSON BOWS. HE BOWS TO
HER TOO AND SHE SIMPERS BACK.
THE POISSONS GO TO TALK TO MA
COUPEAU. CLEMENCE FOLLOWS
BEHIND LERAT.

MME LERAT: (HANDING OVER A SMALL PLANT) There you are, Gervaise. Happy saints' day.

CLEMENCE: Happy saints' day.

MME LERAT: (QUIETLY TO GERVAISE) Who's the imposing gentleman who bowed to me just now?

GERVAISE: Madame Poisson's husband - the policeman.

MME LERAT: (SIGHS) Married - wouldn't you know it?

71

	Mmm, the smell's heaven. Makes a change from dirty washing, doesn't it?
VIRGINIE:	I've not eaten for two days so as to leave room, Gervaise.
CLEMENCE:	(LOUDLY) Oh, I've done better than that. I've done what the English do. Taken an enema to clear myself.
POISSON:	(GRAVELY) There's another useful English custom too, mademoiselle.
CLEMENCE:	(SAUCILY) Is there now?
POISSON:	Yes, they squeeze themselves in a door after each course. It allows them to go on eating for up to twelve hours without upsetting their stomachs.
MME LERAT:	Well, I don't think we'll need the door to get us through tonight's spread. I reckon we'll clean the plates so thoroughly you won't even need to wash them, Gervaise. There's nothing like a nice juicy piece of meat - if you take my meaning.

CLEMENCE GIGGLES.
GOUJET HAS NOW ENTERED WITH
A ROSE TREE.
GERVAISE GOES OVER TO HIM. HE
HANDS HER THE PLANT SILENTLY.

GERVAISE:	Oh, Monsieur Goujet, it's lovely.
GOUJET:	(EMBARRASSED) It's nothing, really.

A   PAUSE   OF   ANTICIPATION.
GERVAISE PUTS DOWN THE BUSH.

GERVAISE:	Coupeau was due back at six. It seemed best to get him out of the way while we finished the preparations. But I expect he's got held up somewhere.
VIRGINIE:	Is everybody else here then?
GERVAISE:	Not quite.

AND ON CUE THE LORILLEUXS
FINALLY APPEAR.
MA COUPEAU TAKES UP HER POST
TO SEE THEIR REACTION.
THEY WAIT ON THE THRESHOLD.
GERVAISE GOES OVER AND KISSES
MME LORILLEUX.

GERVAISE: Come on in, do. No hard feelings, eh?
                Not any more.
MME L: I'm sure Lorilleux and I will try our best
                to bury the past.

                THEY ENTER AND SEE THE
                SPREAD. THEIR FACES FALL.

GERVAISE: Do take your places everybody.
MA C: (WHISPERING TO GERVAISE) They
                looked ill both of them.
GERVAISE: It's painful to see people that envious.

                EVERYONE IS SEATED. AN AIR OF
                EXPECTANCY.

GERVAISE: If only Coupeau'd hurry up, we could
                start.
LORILLEUX: Well, well, we'll have cold soup. You
                must learn to keep an eye on that
                husband of yours.
MME L: Coupeau's always late. Except when he
                dined with us, of course.
GERVAISE: What is the time?
POISSON: (CONSULTING HIS WATCH) It's half
                past six.

                AN AWKWARD PAUSE. THEN
                GERVAISE RISES.

73

GERVAISE: I'll go and fetch him. He's just round the corner.

LIGHTS. THE OTHERS WAITING AT THE TABLE FREEZE.
COUPEAU IS REVEALED DRINKING. AND WITH HIS BACK TO US, APART, LANTIER. GERVAISE GOES UP TO COUPEAU.

GERVAISE: Everyone's waiting.
COUPEAU: I've got business to settle.
GERVAISE: That's spirits you're drinking.
COUPEAU: So? I've got things on my mind.
GERVAISE: (TRYING TO MOVE HIM AWAY) Is it so important just now?
COUPEAU: (DANGEROUSLY) Yes, it is, as a matter of fact. There's a bloke over the other side of the bar you know very well. (PAUSE) And don't come the innocent with me, you know very well who I mean.
GERVAISE: I don't. Now -
COUPEAU: Oh, I think you do. It's not me you're all dolled up for, is it, it's him.
GERVAISE: (GETTING UNEASY) You're crazy.
COUPEAU: Well, let me tell you something, if I meet him face to face, there'll be blood on the floor and it won't be mine.
GERVAISE: Coupeau, please, the meal's ready. Come along, please. Don't spoil everything.

AND SHE MANAGES TO DRAG HIM FINALLY AWAY.
AS THEY LEAVE, LANTIER TURNS TO WATCH THEM GO.
LIGHTS. THE GUESTS WAIT.

74

COUPEAU AND GERVAISE ENTER.
THE GUESTS UNFREEZE AND
CHEER.
COUPEAU IS SUDDENLY ALL
SMILES AND KISSES HIS WIFE.

COUPEAU: Let battle commence.

THE PLATES ARE IMMEDIATELY
STRUCK AND REPLACED BY
EMPTY ONES.
THE MEAL IS OVER.

VIRGINIE: What a feast.
CLEMENCE: I'm full to bust.
MME LERAT: What a spread.
POISSON: I can hardly move.
MME L: Very nice, Gervaise. Goose is never my
                favourite but very nice all the same.
GOUJET;   You're a wonderful cook, Madame
                Gervaise.
LORILLEUX: I've eaten too much.
MA C: I'm stuffed.
COUPEAU: You know, Gervaise, I reckon this is the
                hardest day's work this worktable's ever
                seen.

MUCH LAUGHTER. POISSON RISES.

POISSON: I drink the health of the lady of the house.
VIRGINIE: May she reign here for fifty years.
GERVAISE: And may you all be with me then to
                celebrate.

THE TOAST IS GIVEN.

COUPEAU: Another bottle of wine, ma.
CLEMENCE: And a song. I like a nice song.

75

MA C: A nice sad song. (TURNING TO MME LERAT) Come on, Julie, give us 'The Motherless Child'.

MME LERAT FEIGNS RELUCTANCE BUT THE OTHERS INSIST. FINALLY SHE GIVES IN AND AFTER MUCH PREPARATION BEGINS:

When a poor little child suffers Mother's rejection.,
Turned out from her home, left to wander abroad,
God sees from his throne and sends down his protection:
The motherless child is the child of the Lord ...

THE OTHERS START DRUNKENLY TO JOIN IN:

On a cold winter's night, while a blizzard was blowing,
A poor little girl ran away from her home;
Her father was dead, and her mother's mind going:
She rushed out all heedless to wander alone.

THE ATMOSPHERE BECOMES VERY MAUDLIN.
MEANWHILE LANTIER COMES OUT OF THE SHADOWS AND COMES NEARER.
GERVAISE SENSES HIS PRESENCE.
SHE LOOKS AT VIRGINIE.
VIRGINIE GOES OUT AS THE SINGING CONTINUES.

SHE SEES LANTIER, COMES BACK
AND NODS AT GERVAISE.
COUPEAU REGISTERS THIS. HE
ANGRILY THROWS DOWN HIS
GLASS AND THE SINGING STOPS.

COUPEAU: What the fuck's going on?
GERVAISE: Nothing. It's just that -
COUPEAU: It's him isn't it?

HE TURNS AND WALKS AWAY
FROM THE GROUP.
GERVAISE TRIES TO FOLLOW HIM.

GERVAISE: Don't be silly. Please.

BUT HE'S GONE AND GERVAISE
TURNS HOPELESSLY BACK TO THE
GROUP. FURIOUSLY COUPEAU
APPROACHES LANTIER, WHO
TURNS TO FACE HIM.

COUPEAU: Listen, I want a word with you.
LANTIER: Oh, what about?
COUPEAU: You know bloody well.
LANTIER: I don't. But I'm happy to listen...

INSIDE VIRGINIE TURNS TO THE
OTHERS.

VIRGINIE: What's happened to the singing?

THEY START TO SING AGAIN BUT
THEY'RE MUCH MORE SUBDUED:

Of where she was going, the child had no
notion:
She prayed to the Lord with the snow at
her knees,

But the only reply to her saintly devotion
Was the moaning and sighing of wind in
the trees.

MEANWHILE GERVAISE WAITS
TENSELY. AND OVER THE
SINGING, OUTSIDE LANTIER AND
COUPEAU TALK.

COUPEAU: I warn you. Don't come sniffing round
             my wife.
LANTIER: Relax, it's water under the bridge,
COUPEAU: Is it?
LANTIER: She's got you now, lucky girl. And me,
             I'm not short of female company. I'd just
             like to wish you all well in the new
             venture.
COUPEAU: And that's all?
LANTIER: I can see you've made her very happy.

INSIDE THE SINGING HAS AGAIN
BECOME LOUDER AND MORE
MAUDLIN:

All the night long, the Lord watched o'er
his daughter.
But early next morning, they found her
half dead.
Gently and tenderly homeward they
brought her:
They took her indoors and they put her to
bed.

THE TALK BETWEEN THE TWO
MEN CONTINUES UNDER THIS AND
BECOMES MORE FRIENDLY.
COUPEAU PONDERS THEN LEADS
LANTIER BACK TO THE PARTY.

AS THEY ENTER THE SINGING
STOPS AGAIN. A PAUSE.

COUPEAU: This is a friend of mine - Lantier. He's
                come to join the party.

                LANTIER   NODS   GENERAL
                GREETINGS.
                HE   DOESN'T   PARTICULARLY
                ACKNOWLEDGE GERVAISE. BUT
                SHE IS CLEARLY STILL UPSET.

COUPEAU: Now where were we? Get us another
                bottle, ma.
MME LERAT: It's your turn to give us a song now,
                 brother Coupeau.
COUPEAU: Is it now? Then I dedicate it to all my
                good friends here - and to my wife.
LANTIER: (SMOOTHLY) My congratulations to
                you, Madame Coupeau.
GERVAISE: (BARELY SPEAKING) Thank you,
                Monsieur Lantier.

                THEN COUPEAU STARTS TO SING
                'OH WHAT A NAUGHTY BOY'
                HE PUTS A NAPKIN OVER HIS
                HEAD AND ACTS AN OLD WOMAN.

                Every day when I get up
                My guts are really rough.
                I send the fellow out to buy
                A tasty drop of stuff.
                He takes an hour to get there,
                Then, trying to annoy,
                He drinks his fill on the way back home -
                Oh, what a naughty boy.

                THE OTHERS JOIN IN THE CHORUS:

Oh, what a naughty boy! Oh, what a
naughty boy!
Sometimes he swigs the blooming lot,
Oh, what a naughty boy!

My uncle is a cesspool man
Who always likes a treat;
Last time we went to see him
We got cherry stones to eat.
It didn't seem to be enough
For the fellow to enjoy
So he rolled in uncle's merchandise:
Oh, what a naughty boy.

(CHORUS)

COUPEAU ENCOURAGES THEM
ALL TO JOIN IN.
PEOPLE BEGIN TO DANCE SINGLY
AND IN PAIRS, FULL OF GOODWILL
AND BOOZE.
ONLY LANTIER REMAINS SEATED,
WATCHING.
COUPEAU DANCES TENDERLY
WITH GERVAISE.
THEN GRADUALLY THE REST OF
THE COMPANY WITHDRAW FROM
THE SPACE AND RETURN TO THEIR
ORIGINAL CAFE-CONCERT
POSITIONS TO WATCH.
ONLY COUPEAU, GERVAISE AND
LANTIER ARE LEFT.
LANTIER FINALLY RISES. HE PUTS
HIS HAND ON GERVAISE'S
SHOULDER.
SHE TURNS TO FACE HIM
QUESTIONINGLY.

THEN THE THREE OF THEM PART
AND WALK TO SEPARATE
POSITIONS ON THE EDGE OF THE
PLAYING AREA.
THEY STAND THERE SEPARATELY
LIT, LOOKING AT EACH OTHER.
THE MUSIC FADES AWAY.
THE HOUSE LIGHTS COME UP AND
THE COMPANY LEAVES.

END OF FIRST ACT.

ACT TWO

*

THE COMPANY DANCE A
MOCKING CAN-CAN - THEY THEN
DISPERSE TO WATCH THE ACTION.
COUPEAU IS LEFT SITTING
BETWEEN GERVAISE AND
LANTIER. THE MEN ARE
DRINKING.

COUPEAU: Look, it was my idea in the first place
            and I'm sticking to it. You need a nice
            furnished room in a comfortable house.
            And we happen to have a comfortable
            house with a nice furnished room.
LANTIER: I'm beginning to wish I'd never opened
            my mouth.
COUPEAU: You said you liked our place. You said
            you were looking. It's me that's putting
            the two things together and so you can
            consider it settled. The builders are going
            to turn the dirty-clothes room into a
            bedsitter.
LANTIER: I don't like the idea of driving out my
            own son.
COUPEAU: You won't be. Etienne's off to Lille to be
            an apprentice.
LANTIER: But what about Gervaise?
COUPEAU: It's all water under the bridge, isn't it?
LANTIER: Well, it's true she's more like a sister
            now. But I still think I'd be too much on
            top of you.

HE LOOKS TOWARDS GERVAISE. A
PAUSE.

82

GERVAISE: Coupeau's convinced me it could work
               out quite well.
COUPEAU: Well, let's be honest, the money would be
               useful too. The rent's pretty high. I'm not
               always well enough to work these days
               and the laundry, well, it has its ups and
               downs, doesn't it, Gervaise.
LANTIER: I'd be happy to pay up. It's a very kind
               offer. But I feel -
COUPEAU: Oh for Christ's sake, stop buggering
               about. It's agreed.

               A MOCKING CHORUS OF 'Oh, what a
               naughty boy!"
               THEN POISSON (IN HIS UNIFORM)
               AND LANTIER BRING IN A TRUNK.
               GERVAISE GASPS WHEN SHE SEES
               THE TRUNK.

LANTIER: Bit more battered than when you last saw
               it, eh?

               THE TWO MEN REST AND MOP
               THEIR BROWS.
               GERVAISE CONTINUES TO STUDY
               THE TRUNK, PERHAPS TOUCHES IT
               TENTATIVELY.
               LANTIER STARTS TO OPEN IT UP.
               GERVAISE POURS DRINKS.

POISSON: What've you got in there?
LANTIER: Well, for a start, the key to my future
               prosperity - and the future prosperity of
               all my good friends. Know what this is,
               Gervaise?

               HE FLOURISHES A WEIRD HAT/
               UMBRELLA.
               SHE SHAKES HER HEAD.

83

LANTIER: The hat umbrella. Two in one. When it rains, look! (HE DEMONSTRATES) It's a mug's game being a common or garden hatter nowadays. Flogging your guts out for nothing. Me, I'm going for the big time. And, my dear, you and Coupeau, are coming with me.

GERVAISE: (QUIETLY) I'll believe it when I see it.

LANTIER SIPS HIS WINE AND MAKES A FACE.

LANTIER: No offence, Gervaise, but where are you buying this stuff?

GERVAISE: Vigoureux's down the street.

LANTIER: Well, it's lacking in a little - how shall I put it? -finesse. I'll be happy to point you in the direction of something rather superior at not much more cost.

HE TAKES OUT A PILE OF BOOKS.

LANTIER: My private reference library. (WAVING A VOLUME) The Amours of the Emperor Napoleon III. With illustrations. (HE SHOWS ONE TO POISSON) Wearing nothing but the Legion d'Honneur, you notice.

POISSON: (TAKING A DEEP BREATH) You not going to bait me with that. Even Emperors are only human. It's what they represent that matters.

LANTIER: (PULLING OUT A PILE OF NEWSPAPERS) Well, that's true.

POISSON: What the hell's all that?

GERVAISE CONTINUES TO TIDY THE ROOM AS THE MEN TALK.

LANTIER:	My library of cuttings. I've been collecting good articles for years.
POISSON:	And I suppose a good article's one that attacks the Emperor?
LANTIER:	Correct. Shall I tell you what I believe in, Poisson?

WITHOUT WAITING FOR A REPLY, LANTIER LAUNCHES INTO HIS SPEECH. HE PLAYS IT PARTLY TO GERVAISE.

LANTIER:	I believe in an end to militarism and war and the creation of a new spirit of fraternity between nations. I believe in the abolition of all privileges, titles and monopolies. To be replaced by equal wages for all and equal shares in all profits for all. Put simply, I believe in freedom, pure and simple.

PAUSE. GERVAISE IS IMPRESSED DESPITE HERSELF BUT POISSON IS NOT.

POISSON:	(RISING) Well, I can't listen to this rubbish all day. I've work to do.

HE PUTS ON HIS HAT AND LEAVES. LANTIER LEAPS OFF HIS TRUNK.

LANTIER:	Ignorant oaf.
GERVAISE:	(RETURNING TO WORK) I don't know why you don't leave politics alone.

COUPEAU ENTERS WITH ETIENNE.

COUPEAU:	Come on, Etienne. Know who this is?

ETIENNE HANGS HIS HEAD BUT
NODS.

LANTIER: I hear you're off to Lille, Etienne. Well,
              just remember one thing. The worker is
              not a slave but he who never works is a
              useless drone.

COUPEAU: (TO ETIENNE) Go on then. Give him a
              kiss.

ETIENNE ADVANCES SHEEPISHLY.
LANTIER BENDS AND KISSES HIM.
UPSET ETIENNE RUNS AWAY.

COUPEAU: (RUNNING AFTER) Come back here,
              Etienne, don't be silly.

LANTIER AND GERVAISE ARE
ALONE.

GERVAISE: (TENSE HERSELF) He's upset.
LANTIER: Not surprising, I suppose. (PAUSE)
              You've done well for yourself, Gervaise.
              I'm proud of you.

GOUJET ENTERS BUT STOPS WHEN
HE SEES THEM TOGETHER.

LANTIER: You're still a nice-looking woman,
              Gervaise. It's a good thing I'm suited
              elsewhere and Coupeau's my mate.
              Otherwise -

HE LOOKS UP AND SEES GOUJET.
GERVAISE FOLLOWS HIS GAZE.

GOUJET: Madame Gervaise, I -

HE TURNS AND LEAVES.

LANTIER:	He looked upset.
GERVAISE:	That's Monsieur Goujet. He's been very kind to us.
LANTIER:	(SMILING) Has he now?
GERVAISE:	Not like that.

LIGHTS. 'Oh, what a naughty boy' IS HEARD AGAIN.
GERVAISE VISITS MADAME GOUJET.
SHE PUTS HER BASKET DOWN WEARILY.

MME G:	When I want to order my coffin, I'll send for you.
GERVAISE:	I'm very sorry, Madame Goujet, I -
MME G:	At least let's hope it's all there this time, shall we?

SHE STARTS TO LOOK THROUGH THE BASKET.

MME G:	Really, this is too much. Look at this shirt-front. You can see the iron-marks in the pleats. And all the buttons torn off. And look at this bodice. It's not even properly clean. I'm sorry but I'm not paying for that.
GERVAISE:	But, Madame Goujet -
MME G:	They've cut my son's wages again. Money's tight.
GERVAISE:	If you're thinking about what I owe you, I promise –
MME G:	When did you last repay anything? Do you know? Six months ago. Even if you only gave us ten francs a month, it'd be something.

87

GERVAISE:	Well, we've been going through a bad patch at the laundry.
MME G:	(SHAKING HEAD) No, it's more than that.
GERVAISE:	We've got a lodger now.
MME G:	So I've gathered. But is he paying any rent?
GERVAISE:	He's working on a scheme which -
MME G:	All he's working on is a scheme to enjoy himself at your expense. And I've heard uglier things than that. You can imagine how they hurt my son.

GOUJET COMES IN. HE LOOKS PALE AND ILL.

GOUJET:	Mother, please.
GERVAISE:	Monsieur Goujet, I didn't know you were here.
MME G:	He's not been well.
GOUJET:	Mother, I want to talk to Madame Gervaise.
MME G:	Very well.

SHE LEAVES WITH A BEADY GLANCE AT GERVAISE.

GOUJET:	You don't owe me anything.
GERVAISE:	You're ill.
GOUJET:	It's not important. Really it isn't.
GERVAISE:	But it is. You need some fresh air.
GOUJET:	I know a place.

MUSIC. LIGHTS CHANGE. HE LEADS HER OUT OF THE HOUSE. THEY WALK IN SILENCE INTO A LITTLE AREA OF SCRUB LAND.

GERVAISE: (SITTING) It's almost like being in the country here.

                GOUJET NODS. AN AWKWARD PAUSE.
                FINALLY HE MANAGES TO SPEAK.

GOUJET: You've hurt me very much.
GERVAISE: I don't understand.
GOUJET: Oh, I think you do. I just wish that you'd been honest with me about what was going on.
GERVAISE: Honest about what?
GOUJET: I suppose it was bound to happen. You lived together once, didn't you?
GERVAISE: You mean - me and Lantier?
GOUJET: I saw you together that time. Everyone says -
GERVAISE: No, no, it's not like that at all, honestly. I wouldn't lie to you. It's not like that. The day I let that happen, I'll be the lowest of the low.

                HE LOOKS INTO HER FACE AND STARTS TO SMILE.

GERVAISE: You do believe me? (HE NODS) Your mother doesn't like me, I know. We owe you so much money.

                GOUJET SUDDENLY GRABS HER HAND.

GOUJET: Forget about that, please. I want to say something. Something I've been thinking about for a long time. You're not happy. Mother's sure things aren't going well for you. And I can see she's right. (PAUSE) We must go away together.

89

GERVAISE: What do you mean?
GOUJET: Go away. Somewhere far away from Paris. Belgium maybe. If we both worked, we'd soon have a decent life together.

HE LOOKS AT HER EAGERLY. GERVAISE IS LOST FOR WORDS.

GERVAISE: Monsieur Goujet, I ...
GOUJET: Just the two of us. I don't really like being with other people, you see. And I don't like the people I like being with other people either.
GERVAISE: (TAKING A DEEP BREATH) I'm sorry but I couldn't. I'm a married woman with children. You know I'm fond of you. But I'm too fond of you to let you do something so silly. And it would be silly, really. We're much better off as we are. You're somebody very special. I respect you and you've been a great source of comfort to me.
GOUJET: I - I want you so much.

HE SUDDENLY TAKES HOLD OF HER AND KISSES HER.
SHE SUCCUMBS FOR A MOMENT THEN RESISTS.

GOUJET: I'm sorry, so sorry.

HE RUSHES AWAY, TEARS STARTING.

GERVAISE: Monsieur Goujet, Monsieur Goujet ....

BUT HE WON'T COME BACK. SHE
WEARILY PICKS UP HER LAUNDRY
BASKET AND LEAVES.
THREE WOMAN PASS TO THE
MUSIC OF 'Oh what a naughty boy',
THEY FLIRT WITH LANTIER THEN
LEAVE.

**

LANTIER AND COUPEAU MEETING.

COUPEAU: Lantier, I've got a new regular job.
            Starting tomorrow morning.
LANTIER: Great news, Coupeau. It's just what you
            need. It's bad for a man to be sitting
            round on his backside all day. Work
            gives a man purpose, dignity, self-
            respect.
COUPEAU: That's right.
LANTIER: What time do you start?
COUPEAU: I'll have to be up before dawn.
LANTIER: Then I'll get up then too, go along with
            you, see you safely there. I'm seeing
            someone who's interested in the invention
            later on. So this is a great day, a red letter
            day for both of us. This calls for a drink.

            THEY GO OFF. IT'S THE NEXT
            MORNING.
            LANTIER AND COUPEAU APPEAR,
            YAWNING AND SLEEPY. COUPEAU
            HAS HIS TOOLBAG WITH HIM.

COUPEAU: I'm not used to getting up this early any
            more.
LANTIER: You'll soon get back into the routine.

91

THEY PASS A BAR. THEY LOOK AT EACH OTHER AND ENTER.

LANTIER: A bit nippy. Let's have a drop.

COUPEAU: Just the one mind ...

THEY SEE BIBI-LA-GRILLADE SMOKING HIS PIPE.

COUPEAU: My God, it's Bibi. Bibi, have a drink.

BIBI: Don't mind if I do.

COUPEAU: You're looking glum.

BIBI: No, it's that boss of mine. He's full of shit. So I told him to stuff his fucking job.

COUPEAU: Good on you, Bibi.

THE THREE MEN SALUTE AND DRINK.

LANTIER: Mind you, I have to say this, Bibi, no offence, I've been a boss myself and some workmen you wouldn't believe. They leave you right in the middle of an order. All they want to do is skive off and get pissed.

BIBI: The fuckers.

COUPEAU: That's right.

THE MEN DRINK AGAIN.

LANTIER: Course, Bibi, the bosses are full of shit too. They exploit the working man. They bleed him dry for profit. I wasn't like that myself, of course, I was a real friend to my workers but the big bosses...

BIBI: What a load of bastards.

COUPEAU: That's right.

LANTIER SUDDENLY RISES.

LANTIER: Come on, Coupeau, better be going.
COUPEAU: (GRABBING THE TOOLBAG) Christ,
                mustn't be late. Coming, Bibi?
BIBI: Sure.

COUPEAU HAS AN IDEA :

COUPEAU: Hey, Bibi, you need a job, don't you? The
                boss said I could bring a mate along.

A PAUSE. BIBI SHAKES HIS HEAD.

BIBI: No, I'm still off sick. But Mes-Bottes's
                looking for a job.
COUPEAU: Where can I find him?
BIBI: He'll be in Colombe's.
LANTIER: (WARNING) Coupeau -
COUPEAU: Only a minute. It's on the way.

THEY ARRIVE AT COLOMBE'S BAR.
MES-BOTTES RAISES HIS HAND IN
GREETING. THEY ENTER.

MES-BOTTES: Ah, just in time to buy me a drink.
BIBI: I'll get them.

ALL THE FOUR MEN TAKE A
DRINK.

COUPEAU: I've got a job for you at the Bourgignon's.
MES-B: Wild horses wouldn't drag me back there,
                Coupeau. You won't last three days.
COUPEAU: It's that bad?
MES-B: The pits. The boss is always on your
                back. His wife treats you like garbage.
                And they don't let you drink on the job.

93

	By the end of the first day, I'd told them where to stuff their job.
COUPEAU:	Well, I promised Gervaise I'd give it a go today. But if they try any of that shit on with me, they won't see me for dust.

HE RISES. BUT MES-BOTTES PUTS HIS HAND ON HIS SHOULDER.

MES-B;	Hey, Coupeau, we're not going to let that bastard stop us having another drink are we?

THEY BUY MORE DRINK.

MES-B:	You've heard about my award?
LANTIER:	What award?
MES-B:	My title. King of the Boozers.
BIBI:	Yeah, know what he did?
COUPEAU:	No, what?
BIBI:	Ate a dish of live cockroaches.
COUPEAU:	Oh, Jesus.
MES-B:	Mind you, I had a dead cat to chew on while I was doing it.

COUPEAU AND LANTIER PRETEND TO BE REVOLTED BUT THE FOUR DISSOLVE INTO LAUGHTER.

COUPEAU:	(RISING) Look, I ought to be off.
BIBI:	Leave it out, Coupeau.
COUPEAU:	But -
MES-B:	And stop hugging that toolbag like a fucking baby.
LANTIER:	Besides, it's your round.

THE OTHERS AGREE. A PAUSE. THEN COUPEAU SITS.

COUPEAU: It's too late now anyway. I'll go there
                after lunch. Tell them the wife's been
                sick.
LANTIER: That's the spirit.

                COUPEAU RAISES HIS HAND TO
                ORDER DRINKS. THE OTHERS
                CHEER.
                THEY DRINK. THEN THEY'RE ON
                THEIR FEET, MORE FUDDLED,
                LEAVING.

COUPEAU: I'll leave the bag here under the seat. Pick
                it up at midday, alright?

                THE FOUR MEN OUT IN THE
                STREET LOOK AT EACH OTHER.

LANTIER: So where's it to be next?
COUPEAU: Wherever you like, mate.
MES-B: Five hours till lunch, friends.
BIBI: Le Lion D'Or...
LANTIER: Les Deux Marroniers..
COUPEAU: le Moulin de la Galette..
MES-B: Le Cadran Bleu...
BIBI: Les Vendanges de Bourgogne...
LANTIER: Au Capucin...
COUPEAU: Les Lilas ..
BIBI: La Ville de Bar-le-Duc...

                BY THE END OF THE LIST, THEY'RE
                DRUNKER STILL, CLUTCHING
                EACH OTHER AFFECTIONATELY.
                THEY TOTTER OVER TO THE
                FOUNDRY AND CALL UP.

MES-B: Hey, Bec-Sale.
BIBI: Bec-Sale, you old soak.

BEC-SALE PEERS DOWN.

LANTIER:	We're having lunch at Mother Louis's. Coming?
BEC-SALE:	There's a rush job on at the foundry this afternoon.
MES-B:	They can spare you half an hour can't they?
BEC-SALE:	They'll be lucky if I come back at all.

THE OTHERS LAUGH. HE JOINS THEM.

BEC-SALE:	Right, you pissheads, what's it to be?
BIBI:	Trotters with parsley sauce.
MES-B:	An omelette.
COUPEAU:	And a bottle of Mother Louis's best red.

NOW WE'RE AT THE END OF THE MEAL.
COUPEAU TRIES TO DETACH HIMSELF AGAIN.

COUPEAU:	I must get to work. I promised the wife.
BEC-SALE:	Leave it out, Coupeau. I'm buggered if I'm going back to that anvil today.
COUPEAU:	No, I must go, I must -

HE STUMBLES. THE OTHERS CIRCLE ROUND HIM.

COUPEAU:	I must get my tools. From Colombe's. I did leave them in Colombe's didn't I?
LANTIER:	Alright then, we'll all go back to Colombe's.
BEC-SALE:	Have a drink.
BIBI:	Another drink.
MES-B:	Back where we started.

96

THEY STAGGER BACK INTO COLOMBE'S BAR.
THEY ALL FLOP DOWN.
LANTIER PRODUCES A NEWSPAPER TO READ.

BEC-SALE: Comfy here.

MES-BOTTES: A home from home.

BIBI: But with no fucking wife.

LANTIER: (READING) Look at these left-wing phoneys. Once they're voted in, they just arse-lick the government like everyone else. If I was elected, I'd give them a piece of my mind. Fuck the lot of you, I'd say.

BEC-SALE: That's the way, Lantier. Fuck the government.

MES-B: Fuck the left wingers.

BIBI: Fuck the lot of them.

COUPEAU: And fuck politics. Come on, read us the murders.

LANTIER READS:

LANTIER: There's a woman here killed her baby. Drowned it in the public lavvy.

BIBI: Oh, Jesus, do us a favour.

MES-B: Lousy bitch.

LANTIER: No. you've got to remember - it's the bastard who got her in the club in the first place who's to blame. Men treat women really badly, you know.

BIBI: All the same.

LANTIER: How about this then? (READING) 'We are happy to announce the approaching marriage of Elise, eldest daughter of the Comtesse de Bretigny and Raoul, Baron de Valencay, aide de camp to his majesty. Among their wedding presents

97

	are quantities of magnificent lace estimated at more than three hundred thousand francs -"
BIBI:	Fuck that. (SNATCHING THE PAPER) However many lace undies she wears, she's still got an arsehole like the rest of us.
BEC-SALE:	That's right.
MES-BOTTES:	Your round.

THE OTHERS CHEER BUT THEY'RE NOTICABLY MORE LETHARGIC.

BIBI:	No going out in that rain.
MES-B:	Fuck 'em all, I say.
COUPEAU:	Fuck 'em all.
MES-B:	And have this one on me.

THEY FALL COMATOSE AT LAST.
APART FROM LANTIER THAT IS. HE
RISES QUIETLY, FOLDS HIS PAPER,
AND LOOKS AT THE OTHERS.
HE SHAKES HIMSELF SOBER AND
LEAVES.
LIGHTS CHANGE. GERVAISE IS
OUT IN THE STREETS SEARCHING
FOR COUPEAU, CARRYING HIS
TOOLS. LANTIER ENTERS.

GERVAISE:	Any sign of him?
LANTIER:	(SHAKING HEAD) Last seen at the Deux Maronniers the night before last. Sorry.
GERVAISE:	I picked up his tools from Colombe's. I don't suppose he's planning to use them.

SHE STANDS GLUMLY. PAUSE.

LANTIER: Listen, Gervaise - I reckon you need cheering up. How about me taking you down the cafe-concert? (SHE SHAKES HER HEAD) It'll do you good.

GERVAISE: He's never been out more than two nights running before. I don't care any more if he falls down and breaks his neck. I'm sick of wondering when he's coming back.

LANTIER: All the more reason to give yourself a break.

GERVAISE: Why not? He doesn't think twice about me when he's having a good time, does he?

LANTIER: That's the spirit.

GERVAISE SMILES. MUSIC PLAYS.
THEY START TO DANCE.
THEIR DANCING BECOMES MORE INTIMATE.
AROUND THEM THE COMPANY, ALSO DANCING, CREATES THE LAUNDRY.
THE COMPANY LEAVES. GERVAISE AND LANTIER DANCE ON.
MEANWHILE COUPEAU STAGGERS HOME INTO THE LAUNDRY.
HE FALLS AND THROWS UP, DRAGS HIMSELF ACROSS THE ROOM THEN THROWS UP AGAIN.
FINALLY HE MANAGES TO DRAG HIMSELF TOWARDS THE BEDROOM.
THE MUSIC STOPS. THEIR DANCING ENDED, LANTIER AND GERVAISE LOOK AT EACH OTHER.
LIGHTS CHANGE. THEY'RE BACK HOME.

GERVAISE:	It's all quiet.
LANTIER:	Christ! What a stink.

GERVAISE LOOKS ROUND THE ROOM AND THEN GOES TOWARDS THE BEDROOM. LANTIER WAITS.

GERVAISE:	Oh my God... the pig... the filthy pig...
LANTIER:	What's up?
GERVAISE:	All over the bed, all over the room, all over everything. Oh my God, even a pig wouldn't do that. Where am I going to sleep? I can't lie down in the street. I'll have to climb over him.
LANTIER:	(PULLING AT HER) Gervaise, Gervaise..
GERVAISE:	No, leave me alone.
LANTIER:	Come on. You can't stay here. Come with me. Look, he won't be able to hear us.
GERVAISE:	Get off. You'll wake everybody up. We can't do anything here. Not now. Not with my daughter asleep in the house.
LANTIER:	(URGENTLY) Come on, come on...
GERVAISE:	I mustn't, Auguste. (PAUSE) Oh my God, it's his fault I've got nowhere to sleep. It's his fault. He's turned me out of my own bed. I can't do any more.

LANTIER EMBRACES HER AND LEADS HER AWAY.
NANA APPEARS TO WATCH THEM GO.

***

THEN THE TENEMENT GOSSIP STARTS:

Remember how high and mighty old Peg
Leg used to be?
Her and her Finest Quality Work.
All she thinks about now is those two
men of hers.
No wonder she's a fucking wreck.
Out of one bed and into the other.
She's really gone to seed.
She's really let herself go.

Mind you, it won't do her any good.
Her husband and her fancy man are
bleeding her dry.
Not a sou between them that doesn't go
on drink.
She's footing the bill for the both of them.
Well, she can't keep that up for long.
She's really gone to seed.
She's really let herself go.

RAUCOUS LAUGHTER. GERVAISE
IS SEEN SORTING LAUNDRY.

She owes two quarters' rent, you know.
The landlord's talking about turning them
out.
She's up to her eyeballs in debt -
To every shopkeeper in the district.
She's pawned everything worth pawning.
And her business is going right down hill.
No doubt about it.
She's really let herself go.

DURING THIS, OUT OF TIME,
GERVAISE BECOMES COMPLETELY
INTOXICATED WITH THE DIRTY
WASHING.
SHE YIELDS TO THE PHYSICAL
PLEASURE OF LETTING GO.

THE LIGHTS FADE.

LIGHTS UP ON MA COUPEAU
LYING PROPPED UP IN A CHAIR.
SHE IS COUGHING VIOLENTLY.
MME LORIELLEUX SITS WITH HER.

MME L: How are you?
MA C: It's my usual chest. But I reckon it'll do
            for me this time. Not that anybody cares.
            They'd all rather I was dead.
MME L: Not Coupeau surely.
MA C: Oh, I don't have a son any more. That
            bitch has taken him away. She'd beat me
            to death if she weren't afraid of being run
            in.
MME L: And what does Monsieur Lantier say to
            all this?
MA C: (LEANING OVER) I heard them last
            night, Peg Leg and him. Going at it
            ninety to the dozen. Disgusting I call it.
            Coupeau turns a blind eye, maybe he
            doesn't care. But Nana hears it. She
            listens specially which is worse. And that
            woman's in and out of bed with one or
            other of them all the time. As I said to
            Monsieur Goujet, no wonder she's
            looking so clapped out, the tart.

            A   FIT   OF   COUGHING
            OVERWHELMS HER.
            GERVAISE HAS ENTERED TO HEAR
            THE END OF THIS SPEECH BUT
            DOES NOT YET COME FORWARD.

MA C: Oh, sod this cough.
MME L: Well, I suppose if Coupeau doesn't mind,
            it's not really our business. Are you
            alright?

102

EXHAUSTED AFTER HER COUGHING FIT, MA COUPEAU HAS NODDED OFF.

MME L: Looks like you need some sleep, ma. I'll be on my way.

GERVAISE FINALLY COMES FORWARD.
MME LORILLEUX RISES.

MME L: Mother's getting some rest,
GERVAISE: So I see.
MME L: She's fading fast. (PAUSE) You're looking tired yourself, Gervaise. I do hope you're not overdoing things. The shop isn't looking quite what it was either, is it?
GERVAISE: That's none of your bloody business.
MME L: Just trying to be helpful, that's all. Goodbye for now.

GERVAISE WATCHES SILENTLY AS SHE GOES THEN TURNS TO MA COUPEAU.

GERVAISE: You two-faced old cow! What if I have got another man? At least I've known him since I was fourteen and I've had two children by him. That's nothing to what's going on round here, nothing. There's Pierette and her brother-in-law. There's the watchmaker upstairs fucking his own daughter. There's the grocer's wife opening her legs for all and sundry from morning to night. Everybody's at it. And you've had plenty of men on the side

103

when your old man was alive so don't try it on with me.

LANTIER HAS ENTERED DURING THIS.

GERVAISE: Are you listening?

SHE GOES UP AND PUSHES HER. THERE'S NO RESPONSE.

GERVAISE: Don't play silly games with me.
LANTIER: (COMING UP BEHIND HER) Can't you see? She's dead.

GERVAISE LOOKS AT THE BODY IN HORROR.
SHE STARTS TO SOB.

GERVAISE: Oh no, no....

LIGHTS. NANA APPEARS IN A SPOT, DANCING AND SINGING.

NANA: (SINGING) My little pussy loves to play
             Then my mummy locked it away
             But pussy's very clever, there's no doubt,
             When mummy's back was turned, she found a way out.

LIGHTS CHANGE. MA COUPEAU'S BODY HAS BEEN LAID OUT.
A DRUNKEN COUPEAU WEEPS BY HIS MOTHER'S SIDE.
MME LORILLEUX, MME LERAT AND GERVAISE ARE ALSO THERE.
LANTIER ADDRESSES THEM.

LANTIER;	Well, the coffin itself would be twelve francs. But if you want a Mass that'll be ten francs more.
COUPEAU;	My mum... my dear old mum...
LANTIER:	Then there's the hearse. You pay for that according to the ornaments you choose.
MME L:	I don't see the point, I'm afraid. It won't bring mother back.
LANTIER:	Fair enough.
GERVAISE:	No, we ought to do things decently. Even if Ma Coupeau's left us nothing, that's not a reason for chucking her into the ground like a dead dog. We must have the Mass. And a nice hearse.
MME L:	And who's going to pay?
GERVAISE:	We'll pay.
MME L:	You? You're cleaned out. You owe two quarters' rent. The landlord's going to evict you. And still you're trying to impress people.
GERVAISE:	If we all put in thirty francs, it wouldn't break the bank, would it?
MME LERAT:	I wouldn't mind putting that much in.
MME L:	Well, don't look at me. It's not the money I begrudge. I'd pay anything to bring ma back. But I can't stand people showing off in front of the whole neighbourhood. Why not have plumes on the horses and have done with it?
GERVAISE:	Look, I kept Ma Coupeau without much help from you and I'll bury her that way too. (TO LANTIER) We're having the works.
LANTIER:	What are you going about the bailiffs? How are you going to pay the rent?
GERVAISE:	Oh, I won't wait for the bailiffs. I'm sick of it all. Just sick of it.
LANTIER:	(A PREMEDITATED IDEA) There's a way out of this.

GERVAISE:	(STARING What?
LANTIER:	You know Virginie's just come into an inheritance.
GERVAISE:	What's Virginie got to do with it?
LANTIER:	Well, just listen. She's always wanted a shop of her own - a high class sweet shop - and now she's the money, she can have one. She likes this place, I know. And I think I could persuade her to take over the lease and even pay the arrears.
GERVAISE:	(ANGRILY) No! No!
MME L:	Well, I think that's the most sensible suggestion I've heard for a long time, Gervaise. The shop's just been draining your resources, hasn't it, Coupeau?

COUPEAU FINALLY LOOKS UP AND STARES AT THEM.

COUPEAU:	(FUDDLED) What's that?
MME L:	You'd both be much better selling up and going back working for someone else.
LANTIER:	Do you want me just to find out if Virginie's seriously interested in taking over the lease?

GERVAISE DOESN'T REPLY.

MME L:	I expect she'll see sense later on. Better leave the pair of them.
MME LERAT:	Yes, they need to do some hard thinking.

THE SISTERS AND LANTIER LEAVE.
COUPEAU SITS STILL SLUMPED.

GERVAISE:	Well, may be it's all gone but it's not going to Virginie. And ma's still having

her funeral. I just hope somebody'll do the same for me. Eh, Coupeau?

NO ANSWER. BAZOUGE ENTERS DRUNK CARRYING THE COFFIN.

BAZOUGE: Hope I've come to the right place?

GERVAISE TURNS AND STARES AS SHE RECOGNISES HIM.

BAZOUGE: Oh Christ, not another mistake. They told me the coffin was for you.
GERVAISE: (FORCING HERSELF TO REPLY) It is for here, Monsieur Bazouge.

HE TURNS AND FINALLY SEES THE BODY.

BAZOUGE: Oh, I see. It's for the old girl. Sorry, but they'd said somebody had kicked the bucket on the ground floor so I thought ... Well, congratulations are obviously in order for still being with us, my dear. (PAUSE) Mind you, if you change your mind, you have only to tip me the wink. I'm well known as the ladies' comforter.
GERVAISE: (SHUDDERING) That's enough, please.
BAZOUGE: As you wish. But, remember, any time day or night.

HE PLONKS THE COFFIN DOWN IN FRONT OF GERVAISE'S HORRIFIED GAZE.
THE NOISE WAKES COUPEAU WHO STARES DOWN TOO.
LIGHTS CHANGE. NANA AGAIN APPEARS SEPARATELY LIT, SINGING:

107

NANA: Pussy asked my mummy to send
                     A nice little bow-bow to be her friend
                     Mummy said doggies weren't safe for
                     play
                     But pussy found one anyway.

                     THE LIGHTS CHANGE AGAIN. THE
                     COFFIN IS GONE.
                     GERVAISE IS PREPARING FOR THE
                     WAKE. GOUJET IS WITH HER.

GERVAISE: It was good of you to lend us the money.
GOUJET: Don't mention it.
GERVAISE: I think everyone's entitled to a decent
                     funeral.
GOUJET: I'll always be there to help you when
                     you're in trouble. Though I'd rather you
                     didn't say anything about this to mother.
                     She has her own ideas.
GERVAISE: (NODS) But we're still good friends,
                     aren't we?
GOUJET: Of course. (PAUSE) Only you do
                     understand - it's all over between us now.

                     HE TURNS AND LEAVES BEFORE
                     GERVAISE CAN REPLY.
                     MUSIC.   COUPEAU,   LANTIER,
                     VIRGINIE, MME LORRILLEUX AND
                     MME LERAT ENTER AND SEAT
                     THEMSELVES,   CONFRONTING
                     GERVAISE.
                     THERE'S AN OMINOUS SILENCE
                     BEFORE ANYONE SPEAKS.

MME L: Gervaise, I think your husband has
                     something to say.
COUPEAU: Too right I do. Now, listen, Gervaise, just
                     listen to me, just listen. You always get

108

your own fucking way. Not this time. This time you're going to do what I say for once. Alright?

LANTIER: Give up the lease, Gervaise, it makes sense. You're fighting a losing battle.

GERVAISE: Alright, I don't care any more. Take the shop. I'm finished with it. You work your guts out and all for nothing. Take it, take it.

VIRGINIE APPROACHES HER. GERVAISE TURNS FROM HER.

VIRGINIE: No hard feelings, eh? Don't worry. We'll settle the arrears.

GERVAISE: I don't know why any of you think I care so much. I'm sick to death of the shop. I hate the fucking sight of it.

SHE LIMPS ANGRILY OUT.

LANTIER: (QUIETLY) That's settled then.

HE LOOKS ACROSS AT VIRGINIE. THEY ARE ALMOST TRIUMPHANT. MUSIC. THE GOSSIPING VOICES START, MOCK-PITYING NOW:

Poor old Gervaise, she's moved up to the sixth floor now.
Right next to Bazouge -
That's not very nice for her, is it?
Him with his coffins all day.
And she'll miss that laundry.
Must be awful to see it all taken away.
Must be awful when she'd tried so hard.
Must be awful when she'd aimed so high.
But, still, no good crying over spilt milk.

THEY BURST INTO MOCKING SONG:

Poor old Gervaise - she's lost it all.
Her laundry's gone for good - it appears
She's gone up to the sixth -
And her husband's been gone for years!
What can you say? What can you say?
What can you say?
Except - serves her fucking right!

THE MUSIC CONTINUES. GERVAISE DANCES A MAD, ABANDONED CAN-CAN WITH HER TWO MEN - LANTIER AND COUPEAU - PARTNERING FIRST ONE AND THEN THE OTHER. THE OTHERS CHEER THEM ON MOCKINGLY.
THEN THE MOOD EVAPORATES. THE DANCE IS OVER.
GERVAISE WALKS GRIMLY AWAY. EVERYONE LEAVES.

****

MUSIC. COUPEAU IS DRINKING IN COLOMBE'S BAR WITH BIBI, MES-BOTTES AND BEC SALE. THEY'RE ALREADY WELL-GONE.
GERVAISE ENCOUNTERS MADAME BOCHE MEANWHILE.

MME B:	Looking for your old man, Gervaise?
GERVAISE:	Yes, he's going to take me to the circus.
MME B:	I think you'll find he's at Colombe's. Boche has just had a cherry brandy with him.
GERVAISE:	Thanks.

110

SHE STARTS TO MOVE OFF.

MME B: Getting used to your new room are you?
GERVAISE: It's fine.
MME B: Must be nice to be close to your in-laws.

GERVAISE DOESN'T BOTHER TO
REPLY. MME BOCHE LEAVES.
GERVAISE WAITS.
A HUGE DRUNKEN ROAR FROM
THE BAR.
GERVAISE FINALLY PLUCKS UP
HER COURAGE AND GOES IN.
COUPEAU WHO'S WELL GONE SEES
HER COMING AND CALLS ACROSS.

COUPEAU: (BOISTEROUSLY) Hello there, old girl.
                Come and join us.

HE GRINS AND BECKONS HER
OVER.

GERVAISE: It's time to go.
COUPEAU: Sorry, I can't get up.
GERVAISE: (SMILING DESPITE HERSELF) Don't
                be silly.
COUPEAU: No, try and pull me. Go on. Hard as you
                like.

GERVAISE TUGS AT HIM BUT SHE
CAN'T SHIFT FROM HIS SEAT.
THE OTHER MEN CHEER HER ON.
SHE SMILES A LITTLE, GETTING
MORE INTO THE SPIRIT OF THE
THINGS.
SHE GIVES ONE LAST BIG TUG BUT
FAILS TO SHIFT COUPEAU.

COUPEAU: See? You might just as well sit down for
              a bit.

              BIBI PRODUCES A CHAIR.

MES-BOTTES: (LEERING) Unless, of course, you'd
              prefer my lap.
BEC SALE: Or mine!

              GERVAISE SHAKES HER HEAD AND
              SITS. THE MEN FINISH THEIR
              DRINKS.

COUPEAU: Come on, Gervaise, don't be a fucking
              wet blanket. What'll you have to drink?
GERVAISE: (SHAKING HER HEAD) Nothing. I've
              not eaten yet.
MES-B: All the more reason. A drop of something
              will keep you going.
BIBI: Something sweet maybe?
GERVAISE: Look, I like men who don't get drunk. I
              like men who bring home their pay and
              keep their promises.
COUPEAU: (LAUGHING) So that's it, is it? She
              wants her share of the profits. (THE
              OTHERS LAUGH) Well, you can have
              them. I'll buy you a drink.
GERVAISE: (LOOKING AT HIM SERIOUSLY)
              Yes, you're right, it is a good idea. We've
              let the shop go now so let's drink
              everything else away.

              COUPEAU IS UNEASY.
              THE   TENSE   ATMOSPHERE'S
              BROKEN BY BIBI PLONKING AN
              ANISETTE IN FRONT OF HER.

BIBI: Get that down you, love.
BEC SALE: It'll do you the world of good.

112

GERVAISE:	(STARING AT THE DRINK) What is it?
BIBI:	Anisette.
GERVAISE:	(STARING AT COUPEAU) My mother's favourite, remember?
COUPEAU:	Forget all that. Get it down you.
BEC SALE:	It's not strong.
MES-B:	Don't let your old man blow all your cash on his own, love. You get your fair share.

PAUSE. SHE TAKES A SIP. SHE SMILES - AND TAKES ANOTHER SIP. THE MEN CHEER. GERVAISE FINISHES HER DRINK.

COUPEAU: Another drink, madame?

COUPEAU GOES TO POUR BUT HIS HAND STARTS TO SHAKE UNCONTROLLABLY.
THIS FRIGHTENS HIM BUT HE CARRIES ON JOKING.

COUPEAU: Hello, my hand's off on its holidays again. You'd better do the pouring, Bibi.

BIBI POURS GERVAISE'S DRINK. THE MEN WAIT.

COUPEAU: (FIGHTING TO CONTROL THE SHAKES) Now knock it back in one, Gervaise. Bugger this hand. Every swig of that takes six francs out of the doctor's pockets.

A PAUSE. THEN GERVAISE POURS MORE DRINK INTO THE GLASS AND KNOCKS THE DRINK BACK. THE MEN CHEER.
SHE SMILES, SLIGHTLY FUDDLED.

SHE RISES TO HER FEET. COUPEAU RISES TOO, HIS HAND BACK UNDER CONTROL. THEY EMBRACE AND START TO DANCE ROUND.
THE OTHERS LAUGH AND CHEER. THEY ARE DRUNK, FLOATING AND HAPPY.
BUT THERE'S SOMETHING WILD AND CRAZY TO THEIR ENERGY.
THEN GRADUALLY THE MOOD CHANGES.
THE OTHERS DROP OUT. THE LIGHTS CHANGE.
GERVAISE HAS BECOME ILL AND DISORIENTATED.
SHE CLINGS TO COUPEAU WHO'S DRUNK HIMSELF.
THEN THEY FALL TO THE FLOOR.
THEY SIT APART FROM EACH OTHER LOST AND HUNG OVER.
THEY ARE BACK HOME NOW. COUPEAU LOOKS ILL AND BLOATED.

LIGHTS CHANGE AGAIN. NANA ENTERS. SHE IS TRYING OUT A RIBBON.
GERVAISE BUSTLES ABOUT.

COUPEAU: For Christ's sake, where's my dinner?
GERVAISE: Give me a chance. I have to work too, you know.
COUPEAU: And Nana, for Christ's sake, stop tarting yourself up. Fetch me my dinner or I'll shit on your ribbon.

HE SNATCHES THE RIBBON FROM NANA. SHE FIGHTS BACK.

114

GERVAISE:	Oh for God's sake, leave the girl alone. What a pain in the arse he is when he's tight. She's not doing any harm is she?
COUPEAU:	(STILL FIGHTING) You bitch. Listen, my girl, just see how you like it if I dress you up in an old sack for your pains - you little whore.
NANA:	Swine!

SHE TRIES TO SNATCH IT BACK. ANOTHER FUTILE STRUGGLE. DURING THIS COUPEAU BEGINS TO SHAKE BUT STRUGGLES TO CONCEAL IT.

GERVAISE:	(AGAIN INTERVENING) Nana, Nana, you've got something to tell your father, haven't you, Nana?
COUPEAU:	Oh?
NANA:	I've been talking to my aunt Lerat. She says I can go and work for her making artificial flowers.
COUPEAU:	Flower-making eh? Those tarts'll sleep with anybody.
GERVAISE:	Come on now, Coupeau, for God's sake. You're always going on about her needing a full-time job now she's fifteen. And flower-making's a clean, decent trade.
COUPEAU:	I don't care what she does. So long as she brings in some money.

HE MAKES HIS WAY PAINFULLY TO A CHAIR AND SLUMPS IN IT.

GERVAISE:	Don't be upset, Nana.
NANA:	I'm not. He's a pig. All men are pigs.
GERVAISE:	Nana!

BUT NANA RUNS OFF BEFORE
GERVAISE CAN STOP HER.
SHE CONTINUES WITH HER WORK.

GERVAISE: Madame Fauconnier was giving me a telling-off for being late today. I nearly told her to stuff her job. I've been where she is and look where it got me. Now if I want to go out of an evening and have a good time it's my business.

COUPEAU HAS STARTED TO MAKE
INARTICULATE SOUNDS.

GERVAISE: Don't you start again. Nana's as safe with your sister as she'll ever be.

BUT THE SOUNDS BECOME
ODDER. COUPEAU STARTS TO
WRITHE.

GERVAISE: Coupeau -

HE LEAPS UP AND STARTS
SQUASHING IMAGINARY
CREATURES THAT CRAWL ACROSS
THE FLOOR.
HE FALLS TO THE FLOOR, STILL
WRITHING.
GERVAISE WATCHES SHOCKED.
HE CONTINUES TO ROLL ABOUT. A
KEEPER COMES AND TAKES HOLD
OF HIM AND DEPOSITS HIM ON A
WOODEN BOX.

LIGHTS CHANGE. THE
LORILLEUXS HAVE COME TO SEE
GERVAISE.

116

MME L:	So how is that brother of mine?
GERVAISE:	I'm just going to see him.
MME L:	I mean, forgive me, but living opposite, we couldn't help hearing the things he was saying. It must have been awful for you and Nana.
GERVAISE:	The doctor says he's making good progress.
LORILLEUX:	Well, that's something I suppose.

AS GERVAISE LEAVES, MME LORILLEUX CALLS AFTER HER:

MME L:	Virginie's made a lovely job of doing up the shop by all accounts. In quite the best of taste.

LIGHTS CHANGE. COUPEAU DISCOVERED IN HOSPITAL SITTING ON HIS WOODEN BOX. GERVAISE COMES TO HIM.

GERVAISE:	So how are you feeling?
COUPEAU:	Right as rain.
GERVAISE:	How about the inflammation?
COUPEAU:	Gone in no time. I still cough now and then but that's nothing. Not a bad hotel this, is it?

HE GRINS. GERVAISE SMILES BACK.

COUPEAU:	The staff treat you a bit rough sometimes and the manager's a bit of a tartar who doesn't allow booze but there's nothing wrong with the bed.
GERVAISE:	I brought you some oranges.

SHE HANDS HIM TWO ORANGES.

117

COUPEAU: That's nice of you. Makes a change from tisane.

GERVAISE: So you're really feeling better.

COUPEAU: I told you. Right as rain. Now I'm off the booze.

GERVAISE: You said some very strange things, you know.

COUPEAU: (LAUGHING) I bet I did. Imagine. I could see fucking big rats running round and I was running after them trying to stamp on them. And I could hear you calling for me to save you cos some men were chasing after you. Those rats though - like seeing ghosts in plain daylight. (PAUSE) Well, I can remember it all so my brain must be back to normal.

THE LIGHTS BEGIN TO DIM.

COUPEAU: Course I still dream a bit when I go to sleep. I have nightmares. But that's normal. Everyone has nightmares, don't they?

SUDDENLY HE REACHES OUT TO CRUSH SOMETHING.

GERVAISE: (FRIGHTENED) What is it?

COUPEAU: (QUIETLY) Quiet, it's the rats. They're back.

GERVAISE: I don't understand.

COUPEAU: (SUDDENLY FRANTIC) The rats! Look at them! Watch out or they'll attack you! Leave her alone! Get back, you bastards, get back! Stop it! Stop it! And stop laughing at me!

HE STARTS TO STAMP AROUND THE ROOM VIOLENTLY, SHOUTING AS HE DOES SO.
THE KEEPER RUSHES IN. HE MANHANDLES COUPEAU WHO SUBSIDES INTO QUIETNESS BUT STILL PLUCKING AT HIS SKIN AND KICKING OUT. GERVAISE WATCHES HORRIFIED.

GERVAISE: I thought he was better.
KEEPER: He is better. He'll be out in a few days. You'll see.

GERVAISE CONTINUES TO STARE AT COUPEAU. THE LIGHTS FADE.

LIGHTS UP. MUSIC. NANA AND TWO OTHERS GIRLS, LEONIE AND AUGUSTINE, ARE MAKING FLOWERS WITH MADAME LERAT. IT'S A HOT DAY.

LEONIE: Poor Caroline's having a time of it with that boyfriend of hers, she told me last night.
NANA: What do you expect? He's a two-timing bastard.

THEY ALL GIGGLE BUT MADAME LERAT FEELS OBLIGED TO COMMENT.

MME LERAT:	Now I don't want to hear language like that from you, my girl. What would your father say if he knew you said things like that after he's entrusted you to my care?
NANA:	He says far worse.
MME LERAT:	That's not the point.
NANA:	Christ, it's hot. I'll open the window.

AS SHE GOES TO THE WINDOW, A MAN IN HIS FIFTIES VERY RESPECTABLY DRESSED HOVERS OUTSIDE THE WORKSHOP AREA. NANA ADJUSTS HER CLOTHING OSTENTATIOUSLY AS HE WATCHES

NANA:	(WHISPERING TO LEONIE AS SHE RETURNS) He's still there.
LEONIE:	He's been there quarter of an hour.

THEY GIGGLE. MADAME LERAT LOOKS AT THE WINDOW.

MMJE LERAT:	Nana, I've asked you before not to stand by the window. Certainly not where you can be seen by that old lecher.
NANA:	It's not me he's interested in, I'm sure, Auntie. It's Augustine.

SHE AND LEONIE GIGGLE. AUGUSTINE IS THE PLAIN ONE OF THE GROUP.

AUGUSTINE:	It's not. Anyway, I don't like older men.
MME LERAT:	That, my dear, is a mistake. They're more affectionate.
LEONIE:	You can see he's got pots of money.
NANA:	And an eyeglass.

120

MME LERAT: (MOVING DECISIVELY TO THE WINDOW) Anyway, he's gone.

SEEING HER STARING, THE GENTLEMAN MOVES ON.
MEANWHILE NANA WHISPERS TO LEONIE. LEONIE DOUBLES UP WITH LAUGHTER.

LEONIE: Oh, Nana, that's disgusting.
AUGUSTINE: What did she say?

LEONIE WHISPERS TO AUGUSTINE.

MME LERAT: It's very rude to whisper.
NANA: I suppose you want to know what I said.
MME LERAT: (HOTLY) I most certainly do not.

A MOMENT OF PEACE WHILE THEY CONTINUE TO WORK.
THEN NANA PUTS DOWN HER WORK.

NANA: My turn to fetch lunch.

MME LERAT STARTS TO PROTEST BUT THE OTHERS LEAP IN WITH ORDERS.

LEONIE: Shrimps for me.
AUGUSTINE: (LEWDLY) Sausages for me.

THE GIRLS GIGGLE. NANA TURNS TO MADAME LERAT.

NANA: Auntie?
MME LERAT: Fried potatoes, please. You're sure you'll be alright?
NANA: Back in ten minutes.

121

SHE RUSHES OUT EXCHANGING A
KNOWING GLANCE WITH LEONIE.

MME LERAT: That's no excuse for the rest of you to
stop work. I'm just going to pop out
myself for a few minutes.

THEY CONTINUE TO WORK. ONE
OF THEM SINGS A LOVE BALLAD:

Love, come to me soon,
Speak for my heart is thine,
In the joy of our eyes' first meeting,
I shall know, I shall know,
I shall know that thy soul is mine.

MEANWHILE NANA CROSSES THE
STAGE.
THE GENTLEMAN APPEARS AND
RAISES HIS HAT. HE SMILES.
NANA SMILES BACK AND MOVES
ON. THE GENTLEMAN FOLLOWS.
SHE LINGERS AS IF LOOKING IN A
WINDOW.
MEANWHILE MADAME LERAT HAS
FOLLOWED NANA.
THE GENTLEMAN SEES HER
APPROACHING AND WITHDRAWS.

MME LERAT: Come on, my dear, you'd better tell your
auntie all about it.
NANA: There's nothing to tell.
MME LERAT: You can tell he's got money. And he's
distinguished looking too in a way. If
only we could be sure his intentions were
honourable ...
NANA: He just follows me around. He's been
doing it for days.

122

MME LERAT:	Well, if that's all. Just so long as you tell your old auntie if there are any developments.
NANA:	Of course. But don't tell my dad, please. He's been worse than ever since they let him back.
MME LERAT:	So long as you behave yourself then. (PAUSE) By the way, what were you telling Leonie?
NANA:	You really want to know?

MADAME LERAT NODS. NANA WHISPERS. IT'S CLEARLY GROSSER THAN EVEN MADAME LERAT EXPECTED. NANA LOOKS PLEASED WITH HERSELF.

MME LERAT:	But that's disgusting.
NANA:	(GLEEFULLY) Isn't it?

THEY MOVE OFF.

*****

COUPEAU AND GERVAISE ARE SITTING IN GLOOMY DRUNKEN SILENCE.

COUPEAU:	It's just a job for fuck's sake.
GERVAISE:	But it's my job. The only job I know. How dare that cow of a Madame Fauconnier tell me I can't do it any more?
COUPEAU:	You'll find another one. I always do, don't I?

NANA COMES IN HUMMING.

COUPEAU:	Where the fuck have you been?

123

NANA:	Out.
COUPEAU:	Come here. (NANA HESITATES) Come here. What's that on your neck?
NANA:	What's what?
COUPEAU:	Don't get smart with me. That mark.
NANA:	A bruise. Leonie and I were fooling around.
COUPEAU:	That's a love bite.
NANA:	I suppose auntie's been blabbing.
COUPEAU:	You've gone too far even for her.
NANA:	She never stops telling me men are swine. She's got a point.
COUPEAU:	(NOT LISTENING) Flaunting those big new tits of yours all over Paris. Wiggling your bottom in front of every dirty old man in Paris.

COUPEAU HITS HER. NANA
PROTECTS HER FACE.

GERVAISE:	Stop it, Coupeau.
COUPEAU:	Are you going to tell me the truth?
NANA:	Why should I? You believe what you want to believe.

HE HITS HER AGAIN.
GERVAISE TRIES INEFFECTUALLY
TO INTERVENE.

GERVAISE:	Coupeau, please -
NANA:	You're hurting me. Stop it. And don't hurt my face. Please don't hurt my face.

HE HOLDS HER WRIST AND
STARTS TO PULL OFF HIS BELT.

NANA:	I'm not putting up with this.
COUPEAU:	Oh yes, you are. I'll teach you how to behave.

124

NANA: Like you, you mean? Pissed out of your
               head every night.
GERVAISE: Nana, that's enough.
NANA: At least my gentlemen doesn't stink of
               booze and sweat.

               COUPEAU HITS HER WITH HIS
               BELT. GERVAISE TRIES TO
               INTERVENE BUT IS PUSHED ASIDE.
               SHE WATCHES APATHETICALLY
               AS COUPEAU BEATS NANA.
               NANA IS SILENT NOW, TAKING
               THE BLOWS WITHOUT PROTEST,
               JUST PROTECTING HER FACE.
               FINALLY COUPEAU HAS HAD
               ENOUGH. HE STOPS THE BEATING
               ALMOST ASHAMED. A SILENCE.

NANA: (RISING, HOLDING BACK TEARS)
               Finished?

               SHE TURNS AND GOES. A PAUSE
               THEN GERVAISE REALISES WHAT
               HAS HAPPENED. SHE CALLS OUT:

GERVAISE: Nana! Nana!
COUPEAU: She'll be back. (PAUSE) And fuck
               dinner. I'm off to Colombe's.

               GERVAISE CONTINUES TO CALL
               NANA'S NAME AS THE LIGHTS
               FADE ON HER.
               THE GENTLEMAN ADMIRER
               APPEARS WITH A BOUQUET.
               NANA APPEARS. HE OFFERS IT TO
               HER.
               SHE TAKES IT CASUALLY AND
               WALKS ON.

THE ADMIRER STANDS SHOCKED
BY HIS REJECTION.
AND THEN STARTS TO RUN AFTER
HER AGAIN.

LIGHTS ON VIRGINIE IN HER SHOP,
LOOKING VERY SMART.
LANTIER SITTING NEARBY EATING
SWEETS.
GERVAISE APPEARS CARRYING A
PAIL AND MOP.
SHE PAUSES FOR A MOMENT.
THEN ENTERS THE SHOP.

LANTIER: Come on in.
VIRGINIE: I wasn't sure you'd come.
LANTIER: Oh yes, she'll come alright, won't you,
               Gervaise. Even once a week's worth
               having. No good sitting at home feeling
               sorry for yourself because you're out of
               work, is there?
VIRGINIE: The floor's going to need a really good
               scrub, I'm afraid. Customers have been
               bringing their muddy feet in and out all
               morning. That's the price of being busy.

GERVAISE STARTS TO CLEAN THE
FLOOR. THE OTHERS WATCH.

LANTIER: How is the old man by the way?
GERVAISE: He'll be out and right as rain again soon.
LANTIER: Well, give him my best wishes when you
               see him.
GERVAISE: I will.
LANTIER: It's a tough life for all of us. I've had no
               end of trouble trying to get my invention
               accepted. People have no imagination. If
               it weren't for Virginie's support, I don't

126

where I'd be. Oh, and Poisson's too, of course.

HE GRINS AT VIRGINIE. SHE LOOKS AT GERVAISE.

VIRGINIE: It looks a bit different from when you were here, doesn't it?

GERVAISE: It's very nice.

VIRGINIE: Thank you. Well, it has to look nice if you're going to attract the right sort of customers. And we only sell the best confectionary here.

LANTIER: (REACHING FOR FRESH SUPPLIES) And I'll vouch for that.

HE GRINS AGAIN AT VIRGINIE AS HE POPS A SWEET IN HER MOUTH.

VIRGINIE: Mind the woodwork now, won't you? It's freshly painted.

LANTIER: The more elbow-grease you put into it, the more it shines, eh?

GERVAISE CONTINUES TO CLEAN. THE OTHERS TO EAT SWEETS.

LANTIER: Oh, by the way, I bumped into Nana last night.

GERVAISE: (STIFFENING FOR THE FIRST TIME) Oh?

LANTIER: Yeah, I was going along the Rue des Martyrs and I saw someone on the arm of this old man wriggling about and I thought, "I'd know that backside anywhere". So I caught them up and sure enough it was Nana. There's no flies on her. She beckoned me to follow her and then she dumped her old man in a cafe

	somewhere and came and joined me for a chat. She's bleeding the old sod dry if you ask me. Anyway, she gave me a kiss and asked after everybody. Nice to see her, eh?
GERVAISE:	Yes.
VIRGINIE:	Well, no offence, Madame Coupeau, but if I saw her I'm afraid I'd have to cross the street to avoid her. Every day Poisson hauls in girls who are better than she is.
LANTIER:	Well, the meat may be rotten but it's still looking very tasty.

BUT VIRGINIE GIVES HIM A FILTHY LOOK AND TURNS TO GERVAISE.

VIRGINIE:	And can you get a move on there. I don't want my customers wading through a pool of water. Oh, here's Poisson.

POISSON ENTERS IN UNIFORM. VIRGINIE LOOKS UP NONE TOO FRIENDLY.

POISSON:	(LOOKING DOWN) My God, it's Madame Coupeau. How are you?
VIRGINIE:	She's busy. (PAUSE) How about you?
POISSON:	Just got a few minutes so thought I'd drop by.
LANTIER:	(BREAKING THE TENSE ATMOSPHERE) Here, Poisson, I saw your boss, the Emperor, in the Rue de Rivoli yesterday. He looks clapped out. Not more than six months to live I'd say. No wonder with the life he leads.
POISSON:	I suppose you're going to tell me you could make a better job of running the country than the Emperor?

128

LANTIER:	I couldn't make a worse now, could I? He's turned the whole country into one big knocking shop.
POISSON:	Now that's enough, Auguste. Show some respect.
VIRGINIE	Oh, stop it the pair of you. I don't care that for politics.
LANTIER:	Alright, my dear, we'll call a halt. No hard feelings eh, Poisson?

POISSON SHAKES HIS HAND WITHOUT SPEAKING. BUT HE CASTS A BEADY LOOK AT HIS WIFE.

POISSON:	I'll be back around six. Goodbye, Madame Coupeau.

THE MOMENT HE'S GONE, LANTIER AND VIRGINIE START TO LAUGH.

LANTIER:	Every time. All you have to do is mention the Emperor.
VIRGINIE:	(STUDYING HIM) You're getting plump, you know. On my sweets.
LANTIER:	Not just me.

HE POPS A SWEET IN HER MOUTH
AND KISSES HER.
GERVAISE COUGHS.
THEY REMEMBER HER.

GERVAISE:	I was just wondering. Did she say anything else to you?
LANTIER:	Who?
GERVAISE:	Nana.
LANTIER:	No, but it was quite a kiss I can tell you that.

129

HE POPS ANOTHER SWEET IN HIS
MOUTH. THE LIGHTS FADE.

A CAFÉ CONCERT. MUSIC PLAYS
AS THE CROWD GATHERS.
FINALLY GERVAISE AND
COUPEAU ENTER. HE LOOKS A LOT
ILLER.
THEY SIT WITH THEIR DRINKS.

COUPEAU: I'm fed up with combing the streets night
after night for the silly little tart. We
deserve something to cheer us up.

GERVAISE: Well, that's Virginie's money gone for the
week.

THEY DRINK IN SILENCE.
BEHIND THEM A CROWD OF MEN
HAS GATHERED ROUND A
DANCING FIGURE SKIMPILY
DRESSED. IT IS NANA. SHE IS OVER
MADE UP AND EGGING ON THE
CROWD WITH THE
SUGGESTIVENESS OF HER DANCE.
THEY ROAR THEIR APPROVAL AS
SHE DANCES THE CAN-CAN.
SUDDENLY COUPEAU TURNS AND
SEES HER.

COUPEAU: Christ! It's Nana.
GERVAISE: Don't do anything stupid, Coupeau.
COUPEAU: Dance! I'll make her dance.

HE STARTS TO MOVE TOWARDS
NANA, PUSHING THE CROWD
ASIDE.

COUPEAU: Let me through. That's my daughter.

GERVAISE FOLLOWS. NANA NOW
SEES HER FATHER AND MOTHER
COMING TOWARDS HER. FROZEN,
SHE SUDDENLY STOPS DANCING.
COUPEAU GRABS HER BY THE
WRIST.

COUPEAU: Weren't expecting to see us were you?

COUPEAU AND GERVAISE DRAG
HER AWAY FROM THE CROWD.

NANA: Let me go. You're hurting.
COUPEAU: Shut up and come with me. I'm still your
father and I've still got a belt.

THE CROWD AND MUSIC FADE
AWAY.
LIGHTS CHANGE. NANA IS ALONE
WITH HER PARENTS BACK AT
HOME.

COUPEAU: Going with rich old bastards is one thing.
Baring your all in a place like that is
another.
NANA: Mind your own fucking business. You've
just made a fool of me and I don't like it.
It's a good job I've got there.
GERVAISE: A good job! Just take a look at yourself.
Plastered in cheap make-up and half-
naked. What do you think you're doing?

SHE SLAPS NANA HARD.

NANA: Don't you dare. Take a look at
yourselves. You're clapped out both of
you. The drink's done for you. And I may
not know much - but I do know I'm not
going to end up like you two.

131

COUPEAU: (GRABBING HOLD OF HER) Stay
                where you are. You're stopping here.
NANA: No, I'm not. Fuck off and leave me alone.

WITH A SUDDEN WRENCH SHE
BITES HIS HAND, BREAKS HIS
GRASP AND RUNS OFF BEFORE
COUPEAU CAN STOP HER.

COUPEAU: (NURSING HIS HAND) The bitch, the
                little bitch. Christ, I need a drink.
GERVAISE: I'll come with you.
COUPEAU: No, you won't. It's your doing she's like
                that. You spoiled her. Christ, I wish I'd
                never set eyes on you.
GERVAISE: Coupeau -
COUPEAU: Fuck off.

HE HITS HER AND STOMPS OFF.
GERVAISE LIES THERE ALONE.

******

GERVAISE ROLLS OVER SLOWLY
AND THEN LIES STILL.
BAZOUGE COMES IN CARRYING
AN UNFINISHED COFFIN. HE PUTS
IT DOWN CLOSE TO GERVAISE AS
IF IN THE NEXT ROOM.
HE STARTS WORK, SINGING TO
HIMSELF FRAGMENTS OF A SONG :
"There were three pretty girls down by
the river..."

GERVAISE LIES, LISTENING, NOT
MOVING.FINALLY SHE SPEAKS:

132

GERVAISE: Bazouge, Bazouge? Can you hear me,
              Bazouge?

              THERE'S NO RESPONSE. BAZOUGE
              CONTINUES TO WORK.

GERVAISE: Doesn't matter anyway, Bazouge, I know
              you're there. The ladies' comforter. I'm
              alone, you see. I haven't seen him in
              days. I wouldn't mind so much but I need
              some money.

              THE HAMMERING CONTINUES.

GERVAISE: I can't remember when I last ate anything
              hot. I keep dreaming about that goose.
              My birthday goose. (PAUSE) Still,
              maybe he'll come back this evening.
              Bazouge!

              SHE CALLS AGAIN. BAZOUGE
              STOPS WORK.

BAZOUGE: What do you want?
GERVAISE: Nothing. It's not important. (PAUSE) We
              get used to anything, don't we, Bazouge -
              except not eating.

              BUT BAZOUGE IS ALREADY BACK
              AT WORK.
              PAINFULLY GERVAISE WEAKLY
              FINDS HER WAY TO HER FEET.
              SHE WALKS ACROSS. THE
              LORILLEUXS APPEAR, HARD AT
              WORK AS USUAL.
              GERVAISE HESITATES BUT THEN A
              STOMACH CRAMP CATCHES HER.
              SHE ENTERS. THE LORILLEUXS
              LOOK UP UNWELCOMINGLY.

MME L: Oh, it's you. What do you want? (PAUSE) Well ...?

GERVAISE: (SOFTLY) I wondered if you'd seen Coupeau. I thought maybe he was here.

MME L: No, we don't offer enough free drink to see much of him.

GERVAISE: He's not been home for days, you see. I looked for him at work but he wasn't there. I need to buy some things...

PAUSE. THE LORILLEUXS REFUSE TO PICK UP THE HINT.

GERVAISE: You couldn't lend me ten sous, could you? I'll let you have them back tonight.

MME L: But, my dear Gervaise, we haven't got any money. Feel my pockets if you don't believe me. Otherwise, we'd gladly lend you something, wouldn't we, Lorilleux?

LORILLEUX: We would if we could.

GERVAISE NODS. THEN SHE GETS THE CRAMPS AGAIN.

GERVAISE: Just ten sous please. I'll pay you back. Please. (PAUSE) Oh my God, to come to this...

MME L: It's still no, Gervaise. There's no money here. (PAUSE) Perhaps if you'd not been so extravagant when you did have money, you wouldn't be short now. I did warn you.

A LONG PAUSE. THEN GERVAISE TURNS TO LEAVE.

LORILLEUX: Just a moment. (GERVAISE STOPS) There may be gold clinging to your

134

shoes. Looks almost like you've greased them on purpose.

GERVAISE: (AS HE CHECKS) Don't you worry. I've taken nothing.

SHE LEAVES. LIGHTS OFF THE LORILLEUXS.
GERVAISE WALKS SLOWLY THROUGH THE STREETS.
GAUDILY DRESSED WOMEN JANGLING KEYS WAIT ON A CORNER.
A MAN EYES ONE OF THEM AND THEN APPROACHES.
A WHISPERED NEGOTIATION AND THEN THEY GO OFF TOGETHER.
GERVAISE WATCHES.
THEN SLOWLY SHE MOVES TO WHERE THE OTHER WOMAN WAS STANDING.
A MAN PASSES. SHE TRIES TO MEET HIS GAZE AND SPEAK BUT FAILS.
ANOTHER MAN PASSES. SHE FORCES HERSELF TO SPEAK.

GERVAISE: Hello there.

THE MAN STOPS, TAKES A QUICK LOOK AT HER, THEN BRISKLY MOVES ON.
ANOTHER MAN COMES BY. SHE TRIES TO SMILE.

GERVAISE: Hello there, lovey.

THE MAN GIVES HER A SEARCHING LOOK.

135

MAN: Jesus, what next?

                HE TURNS ABRUPTLY FROM HER
                AND WALKS SWIFTLY AWAY.
                PULLING HERSELF TOGETHER,
                GERVAISE TRIES THE NEXT MAN.

GERVAISE: Hello there, lovey.

                THE MAN TURNS. SILENCE.
                IT'S GOUJET. HE DOESN'T
                IMMEDIATELY RECOGNISE HER.
                THEN HIS FACE DROPS IN SHOCK.

GOUJET: Madame Gervaise...
GERVAISE: I'm sorry, I ... I was starving, Monsieur
                Goujet.

                SHE TURNS TO LEAVE BUT
                GOUJET TAKES HER ARM.

GOUJET: No, come with me. I'll give you
                something to eat. (SHE HESITATES)
                Come on.

                RELUCTANTLY SHE ALLOWS
                HERSELF TO FOLLOW HIM.
                THEY ENTER GOUJET'S HOUSE.
                GERVAISE SITS.

GOUJET: My mother's dead. She died last autumn.
                But I've left her room just as it was.
GERVAISE: I'm sorry. (PAUSE) So you're alone now.
GOUJET: Yes. But I don't generally go out much.
                It's just that tonight I'd been sitting by the
                bedside of a mate who got injured.
                (PAUSE) Here's some stew I prepared.

136

HE PLACES A BOWL IN FRONT OF
HER.

GERVAISE: Thank you, thank you. It's very good of
                you.

                GERVAISE   STARTS   TO   EAT
                GREEDILY.
                GOUJET WATCHES HER GRAVELY.

GOUJET: Do you want some bread?

                GERVAISE   NODS   AS   SHE
                RAVENOUSLY   FINISHES   THE
                STEW.
                SHE STARTS ON THE BREAD AND
                AS SHE DOES SO, STARTS TO CRY.

GERVAISE: You were always good to me, Monsieur
                Goujet.

                HE CONTINUES TO STARE AT HER.

GERVAISE: Changed, aren't I?
GOUJET: (QUIETLY) I love you, Madame
                Gervaise. In spite of everything, I swear I
                love you.

                GERVAISE   HAS   STARTED   TO
                CLUMSILY   UNDO   HER   BLOUSE
                BUT   NOW   STOPS,   STRICKEN,
                REALISING THAT'S NOT WHAT HE
                MEANS.

GERVAISE: You shouldn't say that, Monsieur Goujet.
                It's hard for me to bear.
GOUJET: Will you let me kiss you?

GERVAISE NODS. HE KISSES HER
SOFTLY ON THE FOREHEAD.

GOUJET: That's all we need now, isn't it? That's
what our friendship is all about, isn't it?

HE TURNS AWAY, STARTING TO
SOB.

GERVAISE: (RISING) I love you too, Monsieur
Goujet. But it just isn't possible, is it? It'd
kill us both.

GOUJET CONTINUES TO SOB.

GERVAISE: Goodbye.

SHE TURNS AND RUNS FROM THE
ROOM.
THE LIGHTS FADE ON GOUJET.
GERVAISE IS ALONE OUTSIDE. SHE
STARTS TO CRY.
AND THEN THE CRYING TURNS TO
LAUGHTER.
A CRAZY, DESPAIRING LAUGH.

AS GERVAISE RETURNS HOME,
BAZOUGE COMES OUT TO GREET
HER. SHE STARTS WILDLY WHEN
SHE SEES HIM.

GERVAISE: What's up? What do you want?
(BEFORE HE CAN REPLY) Come on,
take me away somewhere I can sleep.
You'll see, I'll never move once I'm there.

BAZOUGE: They came about that husband of yours,
my dear. My partner in alcohol. He's in
hospital again. They want you there.

138

LIGHTS CHANGE. COUPEAU
STANDS HALF IN SHADOW.
A DOCTOR TALKS TO GERVAISE.

DOCTOR: Tell me, did this man's father drink?
GERVAISE: Just a little. Like everybody else.
DOCTOR: And the man's mother?
GERVAISE: A drop now and then. But it was a good family. Hard-working. They had their share of knocks and -
DOCTOR: (STARING AT HER) And you drink too?
GERVAISE: (STAMMERING) No, sir.
DOCTOR: Don't lie to me.
GERVAISE: Honestly, sir.
DOCTOR: It's clear you do drink. Well, just take a look where drinking gets you. Some day soon you'll die like this.

COUPEAU IS REVEALED. HIS BODY
IS TWITCHING LIKE A PUPPET'S.
HE MOANS AND SHAKES. HE
SCRATCHES AND STAMPS.
BUT HE CONTINUES TO STARE
OUT NOT REGISTERING GERVAISE.

COUPEAU: (TALKING TO SOMEONE) So it's you, is it? Now, none of that. Don't make me swallow your hair, for God's sake.
DOCTOR: Who do you see?
COUPEAU: My wife, of course.

GERVAISE WATCHES HORRIFIED
AS HE CONTINUES TO TALK INTO
SPACE.

COUPEAU: Now, don't you try and get round me... I'll give you what for, you slag... Where've you hidden that fancy man of

139

yours, eh? Under your skirt? Bend over so I can see. Christ, it's him!

AND COUPEAU STARTS TO FIGHT A BATTLE WITH AN IMAGINARY OPPONENT.

COUPEAU: I'll show you. Get your hands off me.

BUT COUPEAU IS OBVIOUSLY LOSING THE STRUGGLE. THE FIGHT BECOMES A BATTLE WITH AN EVER MORE POWERFUL OPPONENT - A DANCE OF DEATH.

COUPEAU: He's killing her now, the bastard. Slicing her up with a knife. Her belly's split open. The blood's pouring out. Oh, my God, my God, my God....

HE GIVES A COUPLE OF GROANS AND THEN FALLS TO THE FLOOR. HIS LEGS, HOWEVER, CONTINUE TO TWITCH.

GERVAISE: (KNEELING) He's dead.

BUT THE LEGS CONTINUE TO TWITCH CONVULSIVELY. FINALLY THEY SUDDENLY STIFFEN AND STOP.

DOCTOR: Now he's dead.

GERVAISE STARES DOWN AT THE BODY. SHE DOESN'T CRY. SHE'S ALMOST CALM.

GERVAISE: Yes, he's gone.

AS THE LIGHTS FADE ON THIS, THE
PEOPLE OF THE TENEMENT ENTER
GOSSIPING   OVER   THEIR
INDIVIDUAL BALCONIES:

The policeman found his wife with
Lantier.
Poisson must have known they were
carrying on together.
Well, he does now. He's chucked Lantier
out.
What about Virginie?
She owes two quarters' rent.
Leave it to the landlord to turn <u>her</u> out.
Well, you know who ate all the profits.
Anyway, serves her right.
That'll teach her to have fancy ideas.
That'll teach her to put herself above
other people.
She's lost it all now.
Yes and guess who they say's taking over
the shop?
The tripe woman.
Well, that'll suit Lantier. He loves a bit of
tripe.

RAUCOUS LAUGHTER FROM ALL
OVER THE TENEMENT.
GERVAISE HAS COME IN LOOKING
COMPLETELY DRAINED.
THE TENEMENT DWELLERS MOVE
TO THE SIDE TO WATCH HER.
MADAME BOCHE LOOKS DOWN.

MME B: How's the old man?
GERVAISE: He's gone.
MME B: Was he dancing like the last time?

141

GERVAISE: He was dancing all the time.
MME B: Come on, Gervaise, show us.

             THE REST OF THE TENEMENT
             ROARS APPROVAL.
             GERVAISE HESITATES.
             THEN SOMEBODY THROWS A COIN
             TO HER.
             AND ANOTHER COIN.
             GERVAISE LOOKS AT THEN AND
             THEN STARTS TO DANCE.
             SHE DANCES AN IMITATION OF
             COUPEAU'S DANCE OF DEATH.
             MORE COINS FOLLOW.
             SHE CONTINUES TO DANCE.
             FINALLY SHE STOPS.
             A BRIEF CHEER THEN THE CROWD
             GOES.

             THE LIGHTS DIM. GERVAISE SINKS
             TO THE FLOOR.
             SHE ROLLS OVER AND OVER
             SLOWLY.
             NANA ENTERS IN A BEAUTIFUL
             CAN-CAN DRESS.
             HER MOTHER ROLLS TOWARDS
             HER. HER BODY RESTS AGAINST
             NANA FOR A MOMENT BUT NANA
             CARRIES ON, PUSHING HER
             CASUALLY ASIDE.
             GERVAISE'S BODY CONTINUES TO
             ROLL.
             THEN BAZOUGE ENTERS SLOWLY
             AND LIFTS HER DEAD BODY UP.

BAZOUGE: Oh well, she got there in the end. After
             all, there's no need to hurry, there's plenty
             of room for everybody. But then some
             want to go, some don't. This one didn't at

142

first but then changed her mind somewhere along the way. Gently does it.

HE LOOKS DOWN AT HER.

BAZOUGE: You're all right now, my dear. Sleep sound.

HE STARTS TO SLOWLY CARRY GERVAISE OFF.
AS HE DOES, LOUD CAN-CAN MUSIC STARTS.
NANA, ISOLATED IN BRIGHT LIGHT, DANCES A CAN-CAN TO THE ACCLAIM OF THE WATCHERS BACK IN THEIR CAFE-CONCERT POSITIONS.
BAZOUGE FINALLY CARRIES GERVAISE AWAY.
NANA CONTINUES TO DANCE.
SHE ENDS WITH A FLOURISH OF HER CAN-CAN SKIRT AND STANDS BRIGHT-EYED STARING AT THE AUDIENCE.
THE MUSIC STOPS.
THE LIGHTS FADE...

THE END